## Meet Mary Kate and Other Stories

Helen Morgan was born in 1921. She lost her sight at the age of twelve, but partially regained it a year later. She learned braille and trained as a shorthand typist for the blind, but her ambition was always to write and she spent most of her early years working on short stories and poetry. She married in 1954 and had three children.

Shirley Hughes studied at Liverpool Art School and the Ruskin School of Fine Art, Oxford. From the 1950s she worked as a freelance illustrator of other authors' books. She began to write and design picture books when she had a young family of her own. She is best known for series like the *Lucy and Tom* books and the *Alfie and Annie Rose* books. She has won several awards including the Kate Greenaway Award and the Eleanor Farjeon Award for her services to children's literature.

# HELEN MORGAN

# MEET MARY KATE
## and Other Stories

*illustrated by Shirley Hughes*

*faber and faber*

Originally published in separate volumes as
*Meet Mary Kate* in 1963
*Mary Kate and the Jumble Bear and Other Stories* in 1967
*Mary Kate and the School Bus and Other Stories* in 1970
This paperback edition first published in 2000
by Faber and Faber Limited
3 Queen Square, London WC1N 3AU

Photoset by Avon DataSet Ltd, Bidford on Avon
Printed in England by Mackays of Chatham plc, Chatham, Kent

A CIP record for this book
is available from the British Library

ISBN 0–571–20660–3

2 4 6 8 10 9 7 5 3 1

# Contents

For Siân, Megan and Bronwen

## Poor Pussy Pipkin

It was the night before Mary Kate's birthday. As Mummy tucked her up in bed she said, 'This is the last time you'll go to bed three, Mary Kate. When you wake up in the morning you'll be four.'

Mary Kate pulled her old rag doll under the bed-clothes with her. 'I wonder if the postman will bring me any presents?' she said.

'I expect he will,' smiled Mummy. 'Parcels and cards. He'll be ringing the bell tomorrow, you'll see.'

When Mummy had kissed her good night and gone downstairs, Mary Kate cuddled her rag doll and thought about the cake she had seen on the larder shelf. It had pink icing on it. She wondered if there would be four candles for tomorrow. Soon she was fast asleep with the rag doll tucked under her chin.

When she woke up the sun was poking its finger through the gap in the curtains and pointing at something in the middle of the room.

It was a shining, new, blue doll's pram. Mary Kate scrambled out of bed as soon as she saw it. She was so excited she forgot all about her dressing-gown and slippers.

The pram had a blue silk pillow with lace edging and a blue silk cover to match. Under the cover was a pink woolly blanket and a soft white mattress.

Mary Kate fetched her black doll, Bobo, from the window-sill and put him in the pram. Then she put Teddy and Og, the golly, in too and began to push them gently across the room.

She was just going to give the old rag doll a ride when the door opened and Mummy looked in.

'Many Happy Returns of the Day,' said Mummy, hugging Mary Kate. Daddy put his head round the door.

'Hallo, birthday girl,' he said. 'Want to see what I've got for you?'

Mary Kate ran to see what Daddy was holding behind his back. It was a beautiful doll, with curly golden hair. It was wearing a pink frilly dress and white shoes and socks.

'Oh, isn't she lovely!' cried Mary Kate, holding her up for Mummy to see.

Then she took all the old toys out of the pram and put the new doll into it.

'I shall call her Dorabella,' she said. 'May I put her in the garden in her pram, Mummy, like the baby next door?'

'After breakfast,' Mummy promised.

'Good,' said Mary Kate. 'Then Granny will see her as soon as she comes.'

Mary Kate was washing her hands ready for lunch when Granny arrived.

'Happy Birthday, Mary Kate,' said Granny when Mary Kate came downstairs. 'That's a funny-looking baby you've got in your pram, isn't it?'

Mary Kate was surprised. 'That's my new dolly,' she said. 'Her name's Dorabella. Daddy gave her to me. Don't you like her?'

'Hmm,' said Granny. 'She didn't look like a

new dolly to me. I think the fairies must have been at her. I should go and have a look, if I were you.'

Mary Kate ran at once to look in the doll's pram – but Dorabella wasn't there. She was lying on the blue silk cover on the garden seat. In her place in the pram was a little black kitten. Round his neck was a red ribbon and a card which said, 'I come with love from Granny. My name is Pipkin.'

At first Jacky, the dog, didn't like Pipkin at all. He growled whenever the kitten went near him. If Mary Kate made a fuss of Pipkin, Jacky curled up in his basket and sulked.

One morning Jacky was sulking in his basket in the kitchen while the kitten played with one of his biscuits, patting it across the floor with his little velvety paw and then pouncing on it, pretending it was a mouse.

Mummy was washing up the breakfast things and Mary Kate was drying the spoons for her. Suddenly Pipkin sent the biscuit rolling right across the kitchen. It stopped near Jacky's basket and Jacky jumped out and ate it.

'Oh, poor pussy Pipkin!' said Mummy. 'We shall have to buy you a rubber mouse to play with. Jacky won't be able to eat *that*!'

'I'll give him my old rag doll,' Mary Kate said. 'She really is very shabby now and she's so old that her face is all rubbed off.'

'Well,' said Mummy, 'if you're quite *sure* you don't want her any more . . .'

'I'm *quite* sure,' Mary Kate told her. 'I don't take her to bed now, not since Auntie Peggy sent me my cuddly Panda for my birthday. Pussy Pipkin can have her. I'll fetch her now,' and she went upstairs to find the rag doll.

Pipkin sniffed at the doll uncertainly. Then he patted her face with his curled-up paw. When he found she wouldn't play with him he opened his little pink mouth and bit her!

Jacky crouched in his basket watching the kitten. As soon as Pipkin came near him with the doll he snatched it up from the floor, dropped it into his basket and sat on it.

'Oh, you bad dog!' cried Mary Kate, taking him by the collar and trying to pull him out of the basket.

Jacky stayed where he was. Mary Kate could not make him move.

'Leave him for now,' said Mummy. 'Give Pipkin some milk. Jacky will soon get used to having him in the house and then he won't be so jealous.'

Mary Kate fetched Pipkin's little dish from the cupboard and put it on the floor. The kitten went to look at it and so did Jacky.

'Go away, Jacky,' said Mary Kate, carefully lifting the blue and white jug down from the table. 'Get back into your basket. This is Pipkin's milk.'

Jacky put his tail between his legs and went under the table. Pipkin began quickly to lap up the milk, flicking little drops all over his small black face. When he had had enough he sat down a little way from the dish and began to wash himself.

Up jumped Jacky and drank the rest of the milk before Mary Kate could take the dish away. Then he went back to his basket, put his nose between his paws and pretended to be asleep.

Mummy finished the washing up and Mary

Kate put away the knives and forks and spoons in the table drawer. Pipkin stopped washing himself and tippy-toed round the kitchen looking for something to do.

Presently he came across the enamel bowl that held Jacky's drinking water. It was a deep bowl because Jacky was a splashy dog and made a mess on the floor if he had his water in a shallow dish.

Pipkin was far too small to see what was in the bowl, so he stood up on his hind legs, put his front paws on the rim and peeped over the edge. He could not reach the water because Jacky had had a long drink that morning and there wasn't much left. Pipkin stretched his neck and put his head right over the side of the bowl.

Jacky sat in his basket, watching him. Then he stood up and went quickly across the kitchen.

He bent his head, put his nose behind the kitten and gave him a push!

'Mia-ow!' wailed poor pussy Pipkin and over the side of the bowl he went, head first into the cold water.

'You bad dog!' scolded Mummy as she lifted up the wet and struggling kitten and began to dry him on a towel.

Mary Kate said nothing. She looked at Jacky and then at Mummy and suddenly she began to laugh.

Mummy laughed too.

Jacky wagged his tail. He was rather pleased with himself.

'We shouldn't really laugh at him,' Mummy said, 'but it *was* rather funny, wasn't it?'

# Quackety Duck Goes for a Swim

One morning at breakfast Mummy said, 'Granny hasn't been feeling very well for a day or two, so I think we'll go and see her this afternoon and cheer her up, shall we?'

'Oh, yes,' said Mary Kate. 'Shall we take her some flowers out of the garden?'

Mummy thought that was a very good idea, so as soon as the breakfast things were washed up she and Mary Kate went into the sunny garden to pick the flowers.

'We'll pick the ones that are growing on the shady side,' said Mummy, 'and I'll stand them in the blue pitcher in a cool place till it's time for us to go out.'

When they had picked a big bunch of flowers and put them in water Mummy decided to make a cake for Granny.

'Could you make a sponge cake with lemon

curd in it?' asked Mary Kate. 'Granny will like that.'

'All right,' said Mummy, 'and if there's time I'll put lemon icing on top.'

Mummy made the cake and it was quite cool by lunch time, so she iced it and put it in the larder to set.

After lunch Mary Kate went upstairs to have her rest and Mummy cleared away and washed up.

Jacky, the dog, was in the kitchen playing with one of his biscuits. He tossed it into the air and caught it in his mouth. Sometimes he didn't catch it and it rolled across the floor. Then he chased it and growled at it and snatched it up again.

When the washing-up was done, Mummy cleaned Mary Kate's shoes and put them under a chair. Then she washed her hands and went upstairs to get ready to go out.

Presently Mary Kate came one-step-two-step hopping down the stairs, dressed in a clean frock and clean socks, but wearing her slippers.

She went into the kitchen, sat down in her

little chair and began to put her shoes on.

She put the left shoe on and pulled the laces tight ready for Mummy to tie. Then she tried to put the right shoe on but her foot wouldn't go in.

'Mummy,' she cried, 'my foot's too big for this shoe!'

'It can't be,' said Mummy and she loosened the laces and tried to squeeze Mary Kate's heel down.

'Push,' she said. 'You must be able to get your foot in more than that, surely?'

'No, I can't,' grunted Mary Kate. 'I can feel the end with my toes. They're all bent.'

'That's very odd,' Mummy said. 'Let me look.'

She took the shoe off and looked inside it. 'There's something in it,' she said, tipping it upside down.

Out fell Jacky's biscuit!

'No wonder you couldn't get it on!' laughed Mummy. 'There wasn't room in it for you *and* a biscuit!'

'Are we taking Jacky with us?' asked Mary Kate when her shoe was tied at last.

Mummy shook her head. 'Granny's cat doesn't like him,' she said. So they shut Jacky in the kitchen and set off down the garden towards the gate that led into the little wood.

Mummy was carrying her basket with the flowers in it and Mary Kate was carrying Quackety, her rubber duck.

The short cut to Granny's took them across a little bridge over a stream and Mary Kate thought Quackety would like to see the real ducks if they happened to be swimming near the bridge.

When they reached the stream they stopped and Mummy looked in her basket for the bag of bread-crumbs she had brought with her.

'Oh dear,' she said as soon as she put her hand into the basket. 'Do you know what I've done – I've come without Granny's cake!'

'Go back for it,' said Mary Kate. 'I'll stay here and wait for you. Perhaps the ducks will come while you're gone.'

'All right,' agreed Mummy. 'I'll be as quick as I can. Don't go on, now. Stay on the bridge till I come back.'

She gave Mary Kate the bag of crumbs, put her basket down and hurried back along the footpath towards the wood and the garden gate.

Mary Kate leaned over the rail of the bridge to wait for the ducks. Presently she saw them swimming slowly round a bend in the stream. She took some crumbs from the bag and dropped them down into the water.

As the ducks came closer to the bridge Mary Kate threw more and more bread down to them. She leaned over the rail to watch them gobbling the crumbs and suddenly Quackety leaped from under her arm and went down, down, down into the water with a splash!

At the same moment Jacky ran on to the bridge, wagging his tail and panting. He jumped up at Mary Kate and began to bark. All the ducks swam quickly away, quacking loudly . . . all except poor Quackety, who was bobbing up and down on the rough water and saying nothing at all.

Mary Kate pushed Jacky away and looked along the footpath. There was Mummy, hurrying towards her and carrying Granny's cake.

'He ran out as soon as I opened the kitchen door,' she called. 'We'll have to take him with us after all.' Mary Kate wasn't listening. She was peering down at the stream. 'I've lost Quackety,' she wailed. 'He jumped into the water when I was feeding the ducks.'

'Oh dear, I'm afraid you *have* lost him,' said Mummy, coming to look. 'I don't think I can reach him, even with a stick.'

She put Granny's cake into the basket and went to the end of the bridge. There was a gap between the rail and the hedge and the bank was not steep. Mummy searched along the hedge till she found the right sort of stick and then squeezed through the gap and slithered down the bank to the edge of the stream. She stooped down and stretched out towards the rubber duck, but as soon as she touched him with the stick Quackety bobbed away from her.

All the real ducks were out of sight by now and only Quackety was left floating on the ruffled water. Every time he came near enough Mummy tried to hook him with the crooked stick but it was no use. He simply would not let her catch him.

At last Mummy stood up and called out to Mary Kate on the bridge. 'It's no good, I'm afraid,' she said. 'I just can't get hold of him.'

'He doesn't want to come,' said Mary Kate sadly. 'He wants to go with the other ducks. Look – he's swimming under the bridge.'

Mummy looked. 'You're quite right,' she said. 'He's quite out of reach now.' She turned away and climbed back up the bank and on to the bridge. As she stooped to pick up the basket, Jacky began to bark. Mummy and Mary Kate looked over the rail and there was the little dog at the edge of the stream.

Just as Quackety swam under the bridge Jacky jumped into the water.

He caught the rubber duck's tail in his mouth and carried him back to the bank. Then he scrambled up to the hedge, struggled through his own small gap and ran on to the bridge. Dropping Quackety in front of Mary Kate, Jacky wagged his tail and shook himself hard.

'Now we've all had a wetting,' laughed Mummy as she and Mary Kate jumped out of the way of the splashes. 'You're a clever dog, Jacky. You shall have a piece of Granny's lemon cake for your tea.'

'Wuff,' said Jacky, pricking his ears and looking very pleased with himself.

Mary Kate bent to pat his head. 'I'm glad you came with us after all,' she said. 'I'd have lost Quackety for ever if you hadn't been here.'

# A Chill and Aunt Mary

Mary Kate was ill. She felt shivery and headachy and her throat hurt. 'I can't eat it, Mummy,' she said, pushing away her breakfast.

'You've caught a chill,' said Mummy. 'Bed's the best place for you. I'll get you a hot-water bottle and you can go straight back upstairs.'

It was nice being back in bed, warm and cosy, but Mary Kate felt miserable because it was the very day Aunt Mary was coming to stay.

'I shan't be able to go for walks with her or show her my toys or my books or my garden or anything,' she sighed.

'Of course you will,' said Mummy. 'You'll be better long before it's time for her to go home again. I expect she'll come and sit with you, anyway, and read to you when you feel like listening. Just now the best thing you can do is to go to sleep and get well quickly.'

So Mary Kate snuggled down under the bed-clothes, cuddling her hot-water bottle in its blue jacket with the red engine embroidered on it, and soon she was fast asleep.

When she woke up the room was full of sunlight. It was very quiet. Mary Kate couldn't think what had happened. Then she remembered.

'It must be quite late,' she thought. 'I wonder if Auntie Mary has come yet? Oh dear, I *do* want a drink. I'll call Mummy.'

Mary Kate called out in a croaky voice. 'Mummy, can I have a drink, please?' but Mummy didn't hear. She was in the kitchen, peeling potatoes.

'Mummy,' called Mary Kate again, a bit louder. 'Please can I have a drink?'

Still Mummy didn't hear her. Mary Kate waited and waited and then she tried again. 'Mummee-ee-ee . . . Mumm-ee-ee-ee.'

There was no answer. 'I shall have to go downstairs,' sighed Mary Kate. She was very thirsty by now and her head was aching again. She climbed out of bed and put on her slippers and dressing-gown. Then she opened her bedroom door and went out on to the landing. She was starting to go down the stairs when she heard the dining-room door open and Aunt Mary's voice say, 'I'll just run up and peep at her and see if she's still asleep.'

'Oh, Auntie Mary,' cried Mary Kate. 'I'm awake. I want a drink. I've been calling and calling, but Mummy didn't hear me.'

'You poor lamb,' said Aunt Mary, coming up the stairs two at a time. She lifted Mary Kate up and carried her back to bed. 'I'll fetch you a drink right away,' she promised, 'and I'll bring you something else, too.' Away went Aunt Mary and presently she was back again with a mug of orange juice and the 'something else'.

It was the little bell from the dining-room mantelpiece – a brass lady in a crinoline skirt.

'There you are, Mary Kate,' said Aunt Mary. 'No more getting out of bed and no more calling and calling and calling and nobody coming. Just ring this bell when you want something and somebody will be here before you can say "Jack Robinson".'

'Thank you, Auntie,' Mary Kate said, putting down her empty mug. 'I think I'll just lie down again now. I feel all wishy-washy.'

'All right, pet,' said Aunt Mary. 'We won't disturb you.'

Mary Kate slept till lunch time. She ate the scrambled egg Aunt Mary brought her and then Mummy came to straighten up the bed and wash her face and hands.

'Auntie has had an idea,' said Mummy, plumping up Mary Kate's pillow, 'and we want to know what you think of it.'

'What is it?' asked Mary Kate, trying to keep quite still while Mummy smoothed the covers. It was rather difficult because a woolly blanket was tickling her nose.

'Well,' said Mummy, 'we thought we'd take your bed down into Auntie's room when Daddy comes home this evening. Would you like that?'

'Oh, yes,' said Mary Kate. 'Then you can leave the door open and I'll be able to see you.'

'That's what we thought,' smiled Mummy, 'and it will save our poor legs running up and down the stairs – and if you want anything in the night Auntie will be there to get it for you.'

When Daddy came home he came straight upstairs, lifted Mary Kate out of bed and wrapped her in her eiderdown, all nice and cosy. Then he carried her down to the little room off the dining-room where Aunt Mary always slept when she stayed with them. He put her in the big armchair with the blue velvet cushions and went to help Mummy with the bed.

Mary Kate sat and waited. Presently Aunt Mary came in, almost hidden behind a pile of blankets and sheets and with a pillow balanced on her head. She looked so funny that Mary Kate laughed and the laugh made her cough and she had to be patted on the back.

Then Mummy arrived, carrying bits of Mary

Kate's bed, and behind her was Daddy with more bits.

While Mummy and Aunt Mary were upstairs fetching the mattress, Daddy began to put the bits of bed together again in the corner by the little window. At last it was quite ready. Aunt Mary put a hot-water bottle in and Mummy put Mary Kate in.

'When you feel well enough to sit up,' she said, 'you'll be able to look out of the window.'

'And when she wants to *climb* out of the window, laughed Aunt Mary, 'we'll know she's better!'

A day or two later Mary Kate *did* feel better. Her headaches had gone and her sore throat was easier. She didn't feel so hot, but she was still rather snuffly. Being in bed began to be rather boring.

'Will you read me a story, please, Auntie?' she asked after breakfast.

'I'm sorry, pet,' said Aunt Mary, 'but it's Saturday, and I'm going to be very busy today. I'll read to you tomorrow.'

So Mary Kate asked Daddy if he would read

to her, but he said he was busy, too. So did Mummy.

Mary Kate pulled the bedclothes up under her chin, feeling rather miserable.

'What are they all busy *at*?' she wondered.

Presently Aunt Mary came in. 'I've brought you a new picture book to look at,' she said.

Mary Kate was pleased. She sat up in bed and looked at the picture book and every time Mummy or Aunt Mary went past the door they called out to her. They were both wearing big overalls and they seemed to have sacks tied round their middles. They had dusters pinned round their heads and they were carrying brooms and brushes and buckets and mops.

'Auntie, what are you doing?' called Mary Kate.

Aunt Mary laughed. 'Secrets,' she said. She had a black smut on her face and her sack pinny was all wet.

There was a great deal of noise going on overhead. Mary Kate could hear bangings and scrapings and bumps and a strange swishing sound.

Then Daddy went by in his hat and coat and Mary Kate heard the front door close.

A little later on he came back and called out from the hall. Aunt Mary, who was in the dining-room, gave a little shriek and shut Mary Kate's door quickly.

'They don't want me to see,' thought Mary Kate. 'Whatever can they be doing?'

The noises upstairs went on all the morning and all the afternoon – scraping and slapping and bumping, and Mummy and Daddy and Aunt Mary talking and laughing. Lunch was just soup and sandwiches and a banana. Every now and then someone would come and look in at Mary Kate and smile a mysterious smile. They brought her a jigsaw puzzle, a cut-out book and two little dolls to dress and undress, but they wouldn't tell her what they were doing.

'I'm sure they're in my bedroom,' she thought. When Mummy came in with her tea, Mary Kate said, 'I know what you're doing. You're spring-cleaning.'

Mummy laughed. 'Not quite,' she said, 'though we *have* done a lot of sweeping and scrubbing. We should be finished by the day after tomorrow. By then I expect you'll be well enough to go up and see what it's all about. Eat up your tea, now, there's a good girl.'

By Monday morning Mary Kate had sniffed her very last sniff, just as Mummy said she would.

'You can get up after breakfast,' Aunt Mary told her when she brought in the tray.

'Good,' said Mary Kate. 'I want to know what the secret is upstairs.'

As soon as she had finished her breakfast Mary Kate put on her dressing-gown and slippers. 'Can I go up and see the secret now?' she asked, going into the dining-room.

'Not till you've had your bath,' said Mummy. 'Auntie is running it now. Up you go.'

So Mary Kate went upstairs to the bathroom. Her legs felt rather wobbly as she climbed and she had to hold on tightly to the bannister rail. Half-way up she sat down. She could hear the taps running in the bathroom and Aunt Mary singing.

'I wonder if I could just peep into my bedroom,' she thought, 'and see what all the noise was about the other day.'

She began to creep quietly up the stairs, but just as she reached the top Aunt Mary came out of the bathroom.

'Come along, pet,' she said, lifting Mary Kate up. 'A quick bath. No ducks or boats or showers with the sponge.'

'Can't I just peep at the secret?' pleaded Mary Kate.

'Not till you're dressed,' said Aunt Mary firmly. 'We don't want you to catch another chill. Your bedroom window is wide open.'

'So it *is* in my bedroom,' thought Mary Kate as Aunt Mary lifted her into the bath. 'Whatever can it be?'

When Mary Kate was bathed and dried Aunt Mary dressed her by the electric fire in Mummy's bedroom.

As soon as her shoes had been fastened Mary Kate asked, 'Can I see the secret now?'

'All right,' laughed Mummy, coming into the room. They all went across the landing and Aunt Mary flung open the door of Mary

Kate's bedroom. 'Hey Presto!' she said.

Mary Kate gasped. It was no longer a pink and white room with a curtained alcove for her clothes and a chest of drawers so tall that she couldn't see the top of it. The walls were the colour of daffodils and the curtains were striped blue and white. The Stripy Tiger mat that Granny had made her was still there, but there was a new mat as well, with a red and white clown in the middle of it.

The new blue chest of drawers and dressing-table were just the right height for Mary Kate and in the alcove was a real wardrobe. She could reach to open the door herself and inside was a row of pretty coloured hangers for her clothes.

All round the room were paintings of Mary Kate's favourite story-book people and when she looked more closely she saw there were other pictures, too. Some of her toys had their portraits on the walls!

'It's Auntie Mary's birthday present to you,' Mummy told her. 'You remember she promised you something else besides the sweets she sent

31

you? Well – this is it. We had to wait till she came to stay with us because she painted the pictures.'

'We shall have to paint your bed blue, too,' said Aunt Mary. 'We'll put you on a camp bed till it's dry and as soon as the smell of paint has worn off you can move back up here.'

'It's lovely,' said Mary Kate, hugging Aunt Mary. 'Now I know why you wanted me downstairs. You couldn't have done it with me up here. What a good thing I had a chill!'

# Mrs Dover's Tubs

It was raining. Mummy had switched on the electric fire in the living-room and she was sitting in her favourite chair reading a magazine. Mary Kate was drawing a house, but she couldn't get it right. She meant it to be the crooked little house that the crooked man lived in, but it wouldn't come out crooked enough. At last she gave up trying and went to look over Mummy's shoulder at the magazine.

There was nothing but writing on the page Mummy was reading and Mary Kate was just going to turn away and find something else to do when Mummy turned over the page.

Mary Kate stayed to look – and there, in bright colours, was a lovely picture of a house and a beautiful garden.

'Oh,' said Mary Kate. 'Isn't that a lovely house, Mummy?'

'Yes, isn't it,' Mummy agreed. 'There are some more pictures on the next page. Look, this is the back of the house.' She showed Mary Kate another picture.

'Oh,' cried Mary Kate. 'Mummy, look – look at this picture!' and she pointed to a small picture in the corner of the page.

'I don't see anything special,' said Mummy in a puzzled voice. 'It's only a picture of a balcony with baskets of flowers hanging from it.'

'Yes, but look what's on the balcony!' cried Mary Kate. 'Do you see? Big tub things with plants growing in them.'

Mummy looked more closely at the picture. 'Well – what's so exciting about that?' she asked.

'It's Mrs Dover,' explained Mary Kate. 'She hasn't got a garden, but she *has* got a balcony. Mummy, couldn't Mrs Dover have tubs, too?'

'Who's Mrs Dover?' asked Aunt Mary, coming in just then with the tea trolley. 'And why should she want tubs?'

'She's a friend of Granny's,' Mary Kate told her, 'and she lives at the other end of the village in the flat over the grocer's shop. We take her flowers sometimes when we go to see Granny.'

Mummy reached for the teapot and stood it down by the electric fire. 'Mrs Dover is very old,' she said, 'and she can't get down the stairs now, so she has to stay up in her flat all the time. Her daughter lives at the back of the shop and looks after her. The flat has a little balcony overlooking the street. Mrs Dover sits there on fine afternoons watching the people. She used to be a great gardener. She has several pot plants on her window-sill, and Mary Kate takes her primroses and bluebells and whatever else we find when we go through the wood on our way to the village, and sometimes we make her up a bunch of flowers from the garden.'

'I see,' said Aunt Mary. 'And you think she could have tubs on her balcony, do you, Mary Kate?'

'Well, couldn't she?' asked Mary Kate. 'There's an old barrel in the garage. I'm sure Daddy doesn't want it. He had two and he cut one in half and made two tubs to put by the front door. Couldn't we cut the other one in half and give the tubs to Mrs Dover?'

Aunt Mary laughed. 'Not so fast, not so fast,' she said. 'Daddy might want the barrel for something.'

'I don't think he does,' said Mummy, 'but we'll ask him when he comes home. I think it's a very good idea, Mary Kate. We'll see what we can do about it. Now I must go and fetch the rest of the tea things.'

When Mummy had gone Aunt Mary said thoughtfully, 'We can't just give your friend Mrs Dover two empty tubs, you know. We shall have to plant them up for her. And they'll be very heavy when they're full of earth. How are we going to haul them up to her balcony?'

'She's got outside stairs,' said Mary Kate. 'They go right up the side of the shop and on to the balcony. George could carry the tubs up. He's very strong.'

'Who's George?' asked Aunt Mary.

'He works in the shop,' Mary Kate told her. 'He carries huge boxes of groceries about and unloads great crates of things from the vans when they come. I'm sure he could manage the tubs. They'll only be little. It's not a very big barrel, you know. Not as big as the one Daddy used for our tubs. Oh, I *do* hope he says we can have it!'

Daddy *did* say they could have it. In fact, he went out that very evening and sawed it in half. Mary Kate, cuddling her Teddy in her newly painted blue bed, heard him and smiled to herself. 'Tomorrow,' she thought, 'I'll help Auntie Mary to fill the tubs with earth and then we'll plant plants in them and take them to Mrs Dover.'

The next morning after breakfast Mary Kate went out to look at the two little tubs. When she saw them she was rather disappointed. They looked very shabby. Aunt Mary thought so too. 'We'll have to give them a coat of paint or something,' she said. 'Let's go and see what there is in the shed.'

There were several tins in the shed with little bits of paint in them. Aunt Mary looked at them all and at last she made up her mind to take the tin with the most paint – and the paint was yellow.

It took Aunt Mary all the morning to paint the two tubs. Mary Kate did a bit, too, but not much, in case she got herself in a mess. When they were finished, the tubs looked much better than they had done before, but Aunt Mary still wasn't satisfied. 'It's too much of a muchness,' she said. 'All that yellow. I'm going to look in the shed again, Mary Kate. You stay here and wiggle this brush about in this jar of turps to clean it.'

So Mary Kate knelt on the path and wiggled the paint brush about in the jam jar while Aunt Mary poked about in the shed again. Presently Aunt Mary came back with a small tin of red paint. It was a new tin. 'We'll use this,' she said, 'and we'll buy Daddy another one when we go shopping.'

'What are you going to do with it?' asked Mary Kate. 'Are you going to make stripes on the tubs? Or spots?'

'No,' said Aunt Mary, laughing. 'You see these two iron bands that run round the tub? Well, I'm going to paint them red.'

'Well, that *is* stripes,' said Mary Kate. 'Two red stripes going right round each tub.'

'So it is,' agreed Aunt Mary. 'And I think they're going to look very nice when they're done.'

They did. Mary Kate was so pleased with them that she ran indoors to fetch Mummy.

'My goodness,' said Mummy, when she saw the tubs. 'You *have* made them look gay. They ought to cheer Mrs Dover up even if they don't have any flowers in them.'

'But they *will* have flowers,' Aunt Mary said, collecting up the paint tins and the brushes and bottles and jars. 'We'll fill the tubs with earth as soon as the paint is dry. After lunch, Mary Kate, we'll hunt about in the garden for big stones and bits of broken brick to put in the bottom of the tubs so that the water will drain properly and not make a nasty puddle on the top every time it rains.'

They filled the tubs with earth the next day and then Aunt Mary said they must look for some plants to put in them.

'We'll fill one of them with pansies,' she said. 'They go on having lots of flowers for a long time and look very pretty. We'll take one or two bits from Daddy's garden for a start and then I'll run down to the greengrocer and buy a few of those big yellow ones we saw last week.'

The tub looked lovely when it was full of pansies. Aunt Mary was rather proud of it. 'What shall we put in the other one?' she asked.

Mary Kate looked at the tub and then she looked at Aunt Mary. 'I think,' she said slowly, 'I should like to give it to Mrs Dover just as it is and give her some seeds so that she can plant them herself and watch them grow.'

'What a good idea,' cried Aunt Mary. 'You *are* a clever girl, Mary Kate. I should never have thought of that.'

Mrs Dover was delighted with her two bright tubs. She planted the seeds Mary Kate gave her, and whenever Mummy and Mary Kate went to see Granny they looked up at Mrs Dover's balcony to see how the tubs were getting on. On fine days Mrs Dover would be sitting there and she would wave her hand to them. Then, one sunny afternoon, she beckoned to them to come up and see her. They climbed the iron staircase to the balcony to see what she wanted.

'I've got something for you, Mary Kate,' the old lady said with a smile. 'Hold out your hands and shut your eyes, now.'

Mary Kate screwed up her eyes and held out her two hands quite flat.

Mrs Dover put something tickly on the palm of one hand and something small on the palm of the other.

Mary Kate opened her eyes. She was holding a toffee and a little posy of mignonette.

'I grew it myself,' said Mrs Dover, nodding towards the tubs. 'It's the first bunch of flowers I've picked from my own little round garden.'

# The Short Cut

At the bottom of the garden was a little wood. It was so small that from her bedroom window Mary Kate could see right through it to the field beyond and the bridge over the stream. There was a winding path through the woods that led from the gate in the garden to the stile in the fence round the field. It was a short cut to the village and to Granny's cottage.

One Saturday afternoon Daddy and Mary Kate were in the garden pretending to do a little weeding when Mary Kate saw something shining in the grass. She bent down to pick it up.

'Daddy, look what I've found!' she called as soon as she saw what it was. 'It's Granny's brooch!'

'So it is,' said Daddy, coming to look. 'She must have dropped it when she came over with the eggs this morning. Poor Granny – she will be worried. She'll think it's lost.'

'We'll give it to her next time we see her,' said Mary Kate.

Daddy looked thoughtful. 'I think I'll take it across to her now,' he said. 'She's had it a very, very long time and she'll be upset at losing it.'

'Can I come too?' asked Mary Kate.

Daddy looked at his watch. 'I don't think there's time,' he said. 'You're supposed to be going to have your hair cut at four o'clock. Mummy will be wanting to get you ready soon. I tell you what – I'll meet you in the village about half-past four and we'll go and have tea in the Bun Shop.'

'Ooh – lovely!' cried Mary Kate. 'I'll go and tell Mummy.'

She waited till Daddy had disappeared round the bend in the path and then she went back to the house to tell Mummy what had happened.

The back door was open, but Mummy wasn't in the kitchen. She wasn't in the dining-room, either. Mary Kate went through the hall and opened the living-room door. Jacky was in there, curled up in one of the armchairs, where he wasn't supposed to be.

'Naughty dog,' said Mary Kate, scratching him behind the ears. 'You know you're not allowed to sit in this chair.'

Jacky took no notice. He was pretending to be asleep.

Mary Kate was just going to push him out of the chair when there came the sound of a loud crash from upstairs and Mummy's voice calling for Daddy.

Mary Kate ran to the bottom of the stairs. 'Mummy,' she shouted, 'what's the matter? Are you all right?' and she ran upstairs as fast as she could. When she reached the top she saw a stepladder lying on the landing.

'I'm all right,' said Mummy's voice from over her head. 'I was just coming down from the loft when the ladder slipped. Luckily I was holding on to the rail that Daddy put up. Go and fetch him, will you?'

'I can't,' said Mary Kate, and she told Mummy about Granny's brooch.

'Oh dear,' said Mummy. 'Now what are we

going to do? I can't jump down – it's too far.'

'Shall I go next door?' suggested Mary Kate.

'There's no one in,' sighed Mummy. 'I heard them all go out an hour ago.'

'Shall I go to the bungalow, then?' asked Mary Kate. 'I won't walk on the road.'

Mary Kate wasn't allowed to go out by herself yet, because buses came along the lane where she lived and a great many cars and lorries too, and the footpath was very narrow. The bungalow was a little way down the hill and there were no more houses between it and the village.

Mummy hesitated. Then – 'All right,' she said at last. 'But if there isn't any one don't go any farther. I shall just have to stay here till Daddy comes back.'

Mary Kate ran down the stairs and out into the garden. She was opening the gate to the road when she remembered something. That very morning the milkman had told her he had just seen the people from the bungalow piling their luggage into their car. They were off on their holiday!

Mary Kate was about to turn back and tell Mummy when she remembered something else. She was supposed to be having her hair cut at four o'clock and Daddy had said he would see her at the Bun Shop – so that meant he wouldn't be coming back home.

Mary Kate looked down the garden towards the gate and the path that led through the wood to Granny's. There was only one thing to do. She would have to go to Granny's by herself and fetch Daddy.

She ran into the house and called up the stairs, 'Mummy, I'm going to Granny's to fetch Daddy.' Then she ran out again without waiting to hear what Mummy said. She opened the gate at the bottom of the garden and went into the wood. It seemed rather dark under the trees after the bright, sunny garden and the little path was twistier than she remembered, and longer too. Then, at last, she saw a bit of green through the trees.

'There's the field,' she thought. 'I shall come to the fence in a minute.'

She followed the path round a big clump of

bushes and there was the stile. Mary Kate climbed up to the step, scrambled over to the other side and jumped down. Soon she came to the bridge across the stream. The ducks were just swimming underneath, but there was no time to stop and look at them today.

'I must get to Granny's as fast as I can,' thought Mary Kate, running over the little humpy bridge. 'Daddy might have gone to the village already to look for Mummy and me. It must be nearly four o'clock by now.'

The path through the field on the other side of the bridge was very rough, but still Mary Kate ran as fast as she could. At last she came to the kissing gate in the corner of the field. She pulled it towards her and squeezed round it. She was in the narrow alley that ran along the back of the churchyard. There was a high wall on one side of her and a hedge on the other.

There were stinging-nettles all along the hedge, so Mary Kate had to go carefully. When she reached the gate in the churchyard wall she found it shut. The latch was so high up that she had to stand on tiptoe to reach it. It was very

stiff. Mary Kate remembered that Mummy sometimes had to jerk it up and down to make it work. She jerked as hard as she could and then the gate swung open so suddenly that she fell through and tumbled down in a heap on the grass. She scrambled up, rather out of breath and grubby, but not hurt. She was just starting off down the flagged path that led to the main gate when she remembered that Mummy had once told her not to run in the churchyard, so she walked as fast as she could, keeping her legs very stiff and hoping it didn't look like running.

The main gate was always open, so out went Mary Kate into the village street. There was nobody about and there didn't seem to be any traffic, but she stopped and listened and looked both ways before she ran across the road and down the lane on the other side.

There was Granny's cottage and there, at the gate, was Daddy.

'Good gracious me!' he cried when he saw Mary Kate. 'Whatever are you doing here?'

'Mummy's stuck in the loft,' panted Mary Kate. 'The ladder fell down and there's nobody to pick it up, so I came to fetch you. I'm not sure if Mummy heard me say I was coming.'

'Oh, dear,' said Daddy. 'Mummy must have been looking for those books I asked her about. I'd better get home as fast as I can!'

Just then they heard the sound of the bus coming round by the church.

'I'll get the bus. Stay with Granny,' said Daddy and he dashed off down the lane to the bus stop at the corner and jumped on the bus.

Mary Kate went round the back of Granny's cottage to the kitchen door and told Granny what had happened. Granny *was* surprised. 'You'd better have a drink of lemonade and your face and hands washed,' she said, 'and then I'll take you to have your hair cut. It's just after ten to four now, so we shan't be very late.'

'Is that all it is?' said Mary Kate. 'I must have come very fast. I ran all the way – except through the churchyard. It *is* a short cut, isn't it?'

Granny laughed and washed Mary Kate's face and hands and tidied her hair.

'There – you'll do,' she said. 'I'll just put my hat and coat on while you drink your lemonade and then we'll go and get *you* a short cut. After that I'll take you home. But don't expect *me* to run all the way! My legs are far too old for that!'

# The Silver Thimble

Mary Kate woke up one morning with the feeling that something rather special was going to happen. She lay quite still for a few minutes, trying to think what it could be. Then she remembered. Today was Saturday and Auntie Dot and Uncle Ned were coming for the week-end.

Mary Kate leaned over the side of her bed and lifted her best doll, Dorabella, out of the doll's cot, and began to dress her. She was just buttoning Dorabella's pinafore when she heard the alarm clock ringing and a moment or two later Mummy went downstairs.

Tucking Dorabella under her arm, Mary Kate climbed out of bed and followed Mummy down.

'Good gracious me!' cried Mummy, when she saw Mary Kate. 'There was no need for you to get up early as well. And Dorabella dressed already!'

'I put her best clothes on,' explained Mary Kate, 'because of Auntie Dot and Uncle Ned. She's wearing her pinafore to keep her frock clean. She can sit quietly on my little chair until it's time to go out.'

'Is she going out, then?' asked Mummy in surprise.

'Oh, yes,' said Mary Kate. 'I told her last night she could go to the station with us to meet the train.'

'Well, I'm afraid I shan't have time to go,' Mummy said. 'I have far too much to do in the

54

house, and I want to make one of Uncle Ned's favourite fruit and nut cakes. Daddy will have to take you.'

'All right,' said Mary Kate. 'May I have my breakfast now, please?'

'Go and put your dressing-gown on first,' Mummy said, 'and tell Daddy breakfast will be ready in ten minutes.'

After breakfast Mary Kate and Daddy went upstairs to get dressed. Mummy cleared the table and washed up and then she began to make the fruit cake.

When Mary Kate was ready except for her hat and coat she sat on a chair and waited for Daddy to finish dressing. He was just fastening his shirt when one of the buttons jumped off and rolled across the floor.

'Oh dear,' said Daddy. 'Where did that go?'

'Under the bed, I think,' Mary Kate told him – and she knelt down to look. 'I can see it,' she grunted, peering under the bed, 'but I can't reach it.'

So Daddy had to go down on the floor beside her and stretch out his long arm for the button.

'Hold it for me, Mary Kate,' he said, 'while I fasten my shoelaces. I shall have to go and ask Mummy to sew it on again.'

When the shoelaces were fastened Daddy went downstairs to Mummy's workbox, took out a needle and threaded it with white cotton. Then he took the needle into the kitchen. Mary Kate followed him, carrying the button.

Mummy wiped her floury hands on her apron.

'I must have my thimble,' she said. 'I can't sew without it. Run and fetch it for me, will you, Mary Kate?'

Mary Kate ran to Mummy's workbox and took out the silver thimble. She put it in her pocket to keep it safe, closed the workbox and went back to the kitchen.

Daddy stood quite still while Mummy sewed the button on his shirt and then he took the needle and cotton and put them away again. Mummy went on making the fruit cake, and Mary Kate put on her hat and coat and waited for Daddy in the hall.

Mummy was putting the cake mixture into the baking tin when Daddy came downstairs again.

'We're off now,' he called, fastening Mary Kate's coat properly and straightening her hat for her. 'We shan't be long.'

'All right,' called Mummy. 'Good-bye.'

'Good-bye,' shouted Mary Kate and, 'Good-bye,' said Daddy, and they set off down the hill towards the station.

They hadn't gone very far when Mary Kate suddenly remembered Dorabella.

'I forgot all about her because of the button,' she said. 'She's sitting in my little chair waiting to be taken out.'

'Oh dear,' said Daddy, looking at his watch. 'We haven't a great deal of time now. Surely she won't mind being left behind just this once, will she?'

'Yes, she will,' said Mary Kate. 'I promised her she could come with us. She'll cry if we don't take her.'

'Oh well,' sighed Daddy, 'if you promised, that's different. You wait here and I'll run back for her.'

Off he went back up the hill, while Mary Kate waited on the narrow footpath. In a minute or two Daddy came running back with Dorabella under his arm.

'You were quite right,' he said, giving her to Mary Kate. 'She looked as though she was going to cry.'

'She's still got her pinafore on,' said Mary Kate.

'Well, you'll have to take it off when we get to the station,' Daddy told her. 'We must hurry now, or Auntie Dot and Uncle Ned will be there before us.'

They hurried down the hill and arrived at the

station just as the train came in. Auntie Dot was looking out of the carriage window and she waved to Mary Kate, who couldn't wave back because she was trying to unfasten Dorabella's pinafore.

Daddy went to find a taxi while Uncle Ned collected the luggage. 'I'm on holiday,' he said, 'and carrying a case uphill is too much like hard work for my liking.'

Mary Kate was very pleased. Dorabella had never been in a taxi before.

Mummy had coffee and biscuits ready for them when they got home and the fruit cake was in the oven beginning to smell spicy and nice.

'I've dropped my silver thimble somewhere,' said Mummy as she poured some milk into Mary Kate's mug. 'Will you see if you can find it for me, pet?'

Mary Kate put Dorabella into her pram and began to look for the thimble. She searched and searched but she couldn't see it anywhere. She had just stopped for a minute to drink her milk when Uncle Ned came into the kitchen.

'Mummy says you're playing "Hunt the

Thimble",' he said, 'so I've come to join you.'

He moved the little cupboard and looked under the door-mat and poked behind the cooker with the broom handle. Mary Kate peered into the peg bag and peeped into the vegetable rack and the dog basket, but they couldn't find the thimble anywhere.

'Never mind,' said Mummy, coming in with the coffee tray and putting it on the table. 'I expect I shall find it when I sweep.'

She moved Mary Kate out of the way and opened the oven door to peep at the cake.

'That smells jolly good,' said Uncle Ned.

The cake *was* good. They had it for tea. Uncle Ned had one big slice and then he had another and then he said he thought he could manage a third.

He pulled the plate towards him and began to cut a slice. Half-way through the knife stuck.

'Hallo,' said Uncle Ned. 'What's this?' He poked in the cake with the point of the knife and something tinkled down on to the plate.

It was Mummy's silver thimble!

'Well,' said Uncle Ned, eating up all the

crumbs he had made, 'I've had cherry cake and coffee cake and seed cake, but this is the first time I've ever had Thimble Cake! Jolly good it is, too!'

# *Boots*

It was the night before Christmas Eve, and Mary Kate and Mummy and Daddy were going to stay with Mary Kate's other Granny and Grandad, who lived a long way away. It had been snowing for two days and two nights and while they were having breakfast Daddy said, 'I think the roads are too bad for us to go by car. We shall have to go by train. We can't get to London in time for the morning train, so we shall have to travel tonight.'

Mary Kate was very excited. She had never been in a train at night before.

In the afternoon they went to London and had tea with Auntie Dot and Uncle Ned. After tea Mummy undressed Mary Kate and took her upstairs. She put her in Auntie Dot's big bed with Teddy and a hot-water bottle in a red woolly jacket.

Mary Kate curled herself up small and tried hard to go to sleep but everything was so strange and different from her own little room at home that she just couldn't.

There was a lamp in the street outside and it shone through a gap in the curtains. Every time a car went by a long broom of light swept across the ceiling and showed Mary Kate all the interesting things in Auntie Dot's room ... the china cats on the mantelpiece, the gilt frame on the mirror, the bottles and jars on the dressing-table and the picture of Uncle Ned on the chest of drawers.

At last Mummy came upstairs and took Mary Kate down to the kitchen. She had a drink of warm milk and three biscuits. Then Mummy dressed her in her coat and hat over her pyjamas and wrapped her in a big coloured blanket.

Auntie Dot carried her to the street door. It was quite dark and the stars were out and there were lights in the houses across the road. In some of the windows there were Christmas trees, gay and sparkling bright.

Uncle drove up in his little green car to take

them to the station. Daddy took Mary Kate on his knee in the front, Mummy climbed into the back seat with the two bags and the suitcase. They waved 'Good-bye' to Auntie Dot and off they went.

The train was already at the platform when they arrived at the station, huffing and puffing and eager to be off. Mary Kate was very surprised when Daddy carried her into their compartment. It wasn't at all like the ones she was used to. It had four beds in it – bunks, Daddy called them. There were two down low and two up high. Daddy put Mary Kate on one of the bottom bunks and Uncle Ned put the case on one of the top ones.

'I'll sleep in the other top bunk,' said Daddy, 'and Mummy can sleep on the other bottom one.'

'Are we going to bed, then?' asked Mary Kate. 'I thought we were going to travel all night.'

'So we are,' said Mummy, 'but we're going to bed, just the same. You're already undressed, so as soon as I've made up your bunk, in you go!'

'I'll *never* be able to sleep,' sighed Mary Kate.

'I thought I could sit and look out of the window and see the night going by.'

Daddy laughed. 'You wouldn't be able to see much,' he said. 'It's too dark.'

'Never mind,' said Uncle Ned, pulling something from under his coat. 'I've been to get something to keep you cosy,' and he gave her Auntie Dot's hot-water bottle, which a kind lady on the station had filled for him.

Mary Kate snuggled down in the bunk with the hot-water bottle and Teddy. 'Good night, Uncle Ned,' she said. 'I'll just have a little nap till the train starts,' and she closed her eyes.

Soon there was a great deal of puffing and chuffing, the guard blew his whistle and the train began to move slowly out of the station. Faster and faster it went through the snowy night towards the faraway place where Granny and Grandad lived – but Mary Kate didn't know anything about it. She was fast asleep.

When she woke up it was morning and the train was pulling into a big station. Mummy and Daddy were already dressed and drinking tea out of their flasks. Daddy gave Mary Kate some of his tea because his had sugar in it and Mummy gave her two biscuits. Then she scrambled out of the bunk and Mummy dressed her. While Daddy folded up the blankets Mummy repacked her overnight bag and then they were ready to go.

Mummy took Mary Kate across the platform to the cloakroom. 'You can have a proper wash when we get to Granny's,' she said as she wiped Mary Kate's face and hands with a damp sponge.

Grandad arrived on the platform as they came out of the cloakroom. 'Come along, come along,' he said briskly. 'I've got the car outside. It's snowing hard and we don't want to stand about in the cold, do we?'

Mary Kate sat in the back of the big car with Mummy and Teddy and she was so excited she could hardly speak.

As they drove out of the station yard a black cat ran across the road in front of them. Grandad slowed down and put his head out of the window to look at it.

'I thought for a minute that was our old

Boots,' he said, 'but it isn't. Boots has got four white feet. That cat's only got three.'

'Boots wouldn't be all the way up here, surely?' said Daddy, in surprise.

'We don't know *where* he is,' said Grandad sadly. 'He disappeared four days ago.'

'Oh, dear,' said Mummy. 'I *am* sorry. I do hope he'll come back soon.'

Mary Kate hoped so too. She very much wanted to see Granny's black cat with the four white feet.

They drove through the snowy countryside for a long, long way and Mary Kate began to feel rather empty inside. At last, half-way up a steep hill, the car turned aside into a drive, and there was Granny's house and there was Granny at the front door to welcome them.

She hugged Mary Kate and took her into the house. There was a lovely smell of bacon and eggs and coffee. 'Breakfast straight away,' said Granny, unfastening Mary Kate's coat.

'Mmm,' thought Mary Kate, smelling the breakfast smell. 'I'm going to like staying with this Granny.'

By tea-time she felt as though she had always

lived in Granny's house, though she didn't really remember the last time she had been there because she had been so small. She trotted about the big kitchen helping Granny to set the table. The curtains were drawn, the lamps were lit and the kettle was singing softly on the stove. Granny brought in a crusty loaf and cut it up. She put the slices into a little basket for Mary Kate to take into the sitting-room, where Mummy and Daddy and Grandad were dozing by the fire.

'Granny says will you make some toast, please,' said Mary Kate, holding out the basket.

Daddy took the two long, shiny brass toasting forks down from their hooks at the side of the fire-place and he and Mummy knelt on the rug in front of the fire to make the toast.

Mary Kate went back to the kitchen to finish setting the table. Granny was just counting out the spoonfuls of tea into the big brown teapot when there came a scratching noise at the window.

'It's Boots!' cried Granny. 'I'm sure it's Boots! He always scratches on the window when he wants to come in!'

She ran quickly to the outside door and opened it. The wind blew in a flurry of snow-flakes and sent the door-curtain billowing into the room. 'Boots! Boots! Boots!' cried Granny into the darkness, but Boots didn't come. At last Granny closed the door and came sadly back to the kitchen.

'Never mind, Granny,' said Mary Kate. 'I'm sure Boots will come back in time for Christmas.'

'He'll have to hurry up, then,' said Granny. 'It's Christmas Day tomorrow. Now, if your mother and father have finished making that toast we'll have our tea.'

Soon after tea Mummy put Mary Kate to bed in Granny's little blue bedroom. 'This is where your Daddy used to sleep,' said Mummy. 'There's a balcony outside the window and an apple tree that he used to climb when he was a boy.'

Mary Kate hung up her stocking at the foot of the bed and Mummy tucked her in and kissed her 'Good night'. Then she opened the window a little bit, drew back the curtains and went downstairs.

Mary Kate soon went to sleep, but it wasn't long before she woke up again. Something was moving about at the bottom of the bed.

'It's Father Christmas!' thought Mary Kate. 'I wonder if he'll put the light on? It's so dark I can't see him.'

She lay quite still and listened. There wasn't a sound. Through the window she could see the low winter stars, very big and bright.

Suddenly, from the bottom of the bed came a rumbly noise.

Mary Kate sat up. 'I know what that noise is,' she said to herself. She moved her feet very gently. The noise stopped. Then something sat on her legs. Mary Kate laughed and put out her hand and touched it.

'I know who *you* are,' she said and called out loudly, 'Granny! Granny! Grannee-ee-ee!'

Up the stairs came Granny and opened the bedroom door. The light from the hanging lamp on the landing shone across the bedroom and there, in the middle of Mary Kate's bed, was Boots!

'Good gracious me,' cried Granny. 'He must

have come up the apple tree, on to the balcony and in through the window!'

'Just as I used to,' said Daddy, coming in to see what all the noise was about.

Granny lifted Boots off the bed. 'I hope he didn't frighten you, Mary Kate.'

'Oh, no,' said Mary Kate. 'I thought he was Father Christmas!'

Daddy laughed. 'Perhaps he is,' he said. 'After all, you never can tell with cats, can you – especially black ones.' He tucked Mary Kate in snug and warm. 'Sleep now, poppet,' he said. 'Stockings don't get filled while children are awake, whether they're filled by Santa Claus or Pussycat Claws. Good night now.' And he closed the door and went downstairs.

# The Jumble Bear

Teddy was lost. When Mary Kate woke up one morning he wasn't in the bed with her. She felt under the pillow but there wasn't anything there except a screwed-up blue handkerchief with little white dots on it.

'I'm *sure* I brought Teddy to bed last night,' she said to herself. She lifted up the bedclothes and looked into the dark cave they made, but there wasn't anything there except her own two legs in screwed-up pink pyjamas.

Mary Kate scrambled out of bed and looked all round the room, but she couldn't see him. There was Og, the golly, on the window-sill with Black Bobo and Ben-Bun, the floppy rabbit, but Teddy wasn't with them. Nor was he on the cupboard by the bed, with Quackety Duck and Wooldog, the knitted puppy Auntie Dot had made for her.

'He must be downstairs in the pram with Dorabella,' thought Mary Kate and went down to the hall to look.

Teddy wasn't in the pram. Nor was Dorabella. She was sitting on the hall table in her hat and coat, waiting to be taken out. Mary Kate put her into the pram and told her to go to sleep and then crept back up the stairs. It was so quiet down in the hall that she knew Mummy and Daddy couldn't be up yet.

Up in her bedroom, Mary Kate opened the door of her new blue wardrobe to see if Teddy was in there on the shelf with the shoes. He wasn't. She looked in the drawers of the dressing-table to see if he was hiding under her clothes, but he wasn't. By this time she was beginning to feel a bit cross.

'Where *is* he?' she said to Og and Black Bobo. They just stared at her. They didn't know where Teddy was, either.

Mary Kate sat down on the Stripy Tiger rug that Granny had made her and pulled all the things out of the cupboard by the bed. She found several other things she thought she had lost but she didn't find Teddy. She was halfway through pushing the things back into the cupboard when she thought of another place to look.

'Under the bed!' she said to herself and lay down on the Stripy Tiger himself and wriggled under the edge of the counterpane into the dark.

Just then, Mummy came in to say 'Good morning'. She didn't say it, though, because Mary Kate wasn't there. At least, Mummy thought she wasn't there, but as she turned to go out of the room she saw one of Mary Kate's legs poking out from under the bed.

'Whatever are you doing down there?' asked Mummy, stooping to pick her up.

'Looking for Teddy,' Mary Kate told her. 'He's lost.'

'He can't be *lost*,' said Mummy, putting Mary Kate into her dressing-gown. 'Just mislaid. We'll find him presently. You'd better come down and have breakfast with Daddy this morning, since you're so wide awake.'

So Mary Kate went downstairs behind Mummy and had breakfast with Daddy, like Saturdays and Sundays. Daddy cut her toast into fingers for her and gave her some of his special marmalade which had big pieces of orange peel in it and wasn't quite as sweet as the marmalade Mummy and Mary Kate usually had. Mary Kate liked it, though she did have to chew hard because of the peel.

By the time Daddy had gone to catch his train and Mary Kate was washed and dressed, she had quite forgotten about Teddy.

'We must dash round this morning,' Mummy said, when the breakfast things were washed up. 'Mrs Sharpe is coming at eleven o'clock to collect the things for the Jumble Stall at the Fête on Saturday. I still have one or two more things to sort out before she comes.'

'Shall I sort out something, too?' asked Mary Kate, not quite sure what a Jumble Stall was.

'Well . . .' said Mummy, thoughtfully. 'If you've anything you don't want that isn't broken or dirty I daresay Mrs Sharpe will take it. They usually have a Toy Corner on the stall. Come upstairs and look through your cupboard while I make the beds.'

Mary Kate didn't say she already *had* looked through her cupboard once that morning! She didn't say what a mess it was in, either. She just followed Mummy up the stairs and went into her bedroom to look through her toys while Mummy went into *her* bedroom to make her bed.

'Did you find anything?' asked Mummy, coming in a few minutes later to find Mary Kate sitting on the floor surrounded by toys.

'Yes,' said Mary Kate, holding up a red and green striped ball. 'This ball. I had two, just the same. One from Uncle Ned and one from Granny. And there are two Red Indians and an engine without any trucks. Will they do?'

'I'm sure they will,' smiled Mummy, beginning to put Mary Kate's toys back into the cupboard. 'There's a big cardboard box in my room. You go and put your jumble into it with mine while I tidy up in here and make your bed.'

Off went Mary Kate with the two Red Indians and the ball and the engine without any trucks. She found the box by Mummy's bed and put the things into it. It was half full of jumble already. Mary Kate thought she would look and see what Mummy had found for the Fête.

She was just trying to open an interesting-looking wooden box when Mummy came into the room. She had something in her hand. It was Teddy!

'Where did you find him?' asked Mary Kate, taking him and looking at him to make quite sure he was still the same.

'Right at the bottom of your bed,' Mummy said. 'All tucked up with the blankets. You must have kicked him down there in the night.'

'I didn't,' said Mary Kate. 'He kicked himself down there. He's naughty. He was hiding to make

79

me hunt and hunt for him. Naughty Teddy!'

She threw him across the room to punish him. She threw him hard, to let him know how cross she was. She threw him so hard that he went out through the open window!

'That was a silly thing to do, wasn't it?' said Mummy, going to the window to look out. Mary Kate followed her. There was a greengrocer's van going down the hill and a motor bike coming up and a bus just passing the house.

'I hope Teddy didn't go into the road,' Mary Kate said. 'The bus will run right over him if he did.'

Mary Kate's house was very near the road. It didn't really have a front garden, only a little sloping bank that Daddy had made into a rockery. Beyond that was the footpath, which was very narrow, and then the busy road.

'*Is* he in the road?' Mary Kate asked anxiously, when the bus had gone by.

Mummy leaned out to look. 'I can't see him anywhere,' she said. 'I'll go down and look properly.'

Mary Kate stayed where she was. She was

never allowed to go in front of the house by herself in case she fell.

Mummy came round the side of the house and down the three steps to the front gate. At the same moment Mrs Sharpe appeared on the footpath. She had come out of the driveway. Mary Kate could just see the back of her little red car behind the big lilac bush.

Mummy came back into the bedroom. 'Mrs Sharpe's in a hurry,' she said, picking up the big box of jumble. 'I'll find Teddy when she's gone.'

She didn't find him, though. She hunted among the plants on the rockery and in the lavender clump and along the footpath and in the road, but Teddy wasn't there. When Daddy came home Mummy told him all about it and he hunted, too. He even shook the big lilac bush but he didn't find Teddy.

'Someone must have come along and picked him up while you were talking to Mrs Sharpe,' he said.

'I suppose so,' sighed Mummy. 'We were all in the hall going through the jumble and the front door was shut.'

'You'd better put a card on the board in the Post Office,' Daddy suggested, 'and I'll ask Jack Turner if anyone's handed Teddy in to him.'

Mr Turner was the policeman. He lived in a neat little house with a dark blue door at the other end of the village. No one had taken Teddy to his house, though. No one took Teddy to the Post Office, either, in spite of the card with big writing on it that Mummy put on the board.

Daddy called at Mr Turner's again on the way to the Fête on Saturday afternoon. It was no use. Teddy wasn't there.

'We'll see if we can find you something nice at the Fête,' Mummy said and she took Mary Kate to the Gift Stall. Mary Kate looked at all the pretty things but she didn't see anything she wanted.

'Try the Jumble Stall,' suggested Daddy, so they did.

'Toys over there!' called Mrs Sharpe from behind a pile of cardigans and pullovers. 'You're early, so you'll have first pick!'

Mary Kate went to the end of the stall. There was her red and green ball and there were the two Indians, standing on the front of the engine without any trucks. Behind them was a pile of books and sitting on top of the pile was . . . what do you think? Teddy! Really and truly Mary Kate's own Teddy, in his red trousers and blue jacket with the button missing!

'I found him in one of the boxes on the roof-rack,' Mrs Sharpe said, when they asked her about it. 'I must have been passing the window

to turn into your driveway when Mary Kate
threw him out.'

'I'll never throw him out again,' Mary Kate
said, hugging her Jumble Bear. 'I don't care *how*
naughty he is!'

# Cake and Aunt Mary

Mary Kate had a cold. Her head was muzzy and her ears were buzzy and her nose was no use at all. She went to bed in the middle of the afternoon and didn't want any tea.

In the night she cried, because her ear was hurting. Mummy gave her a little pill and a cool drink and put a piece of warmed cotton-wool in her ear. Daddy held a square of flannel in front of the electric fire till it was really warm and then put it on the pillow under Mary Kate's head. It was lovely and cosy and the ache in her ear soon went away.

The next morning the doctor came to see her. He looked into her ear with a funny torch thing. It was cold and it tickled. He held his watch up for Mary Kate to listen to, but she couldn't hear it ticking.

'You've got to go to the hospital and see a

specialist,' Mummy said, when she came back into the bedroom after seeing the doctor out. 'Doctor's going to arrange it as soon as you're over this cold.'

So when Mary Kate's cold was quite gone, Mummy took her to the hospital. Granny went with them. So did Teddy. Mary Kate said he wanted to ride in a bus.

The specialist's name was Mr Smiley. 'Hallo, Princess,' he said, when Mary Kate went into the room. He held her hand and talked to her for a bit and then he looked at her ears and her nose and her throat. Then he said she would have to have her adenoids out, because they were too big.

'Come and see me the week after next,' he said. 'On Thursday. Bring Teddy with you, if you like.'

'Let's go and have a peep at the ward,' Granny said, when they came out of Mr Smiley's room. 'Then Mary Kate can see where she'll be coming.'

'And Teddy,' said Mary Kate. 'He's coming, too.'

They went up in the lift to the ward where Mary Kate was going to be. It had nine beds in it and it was quite empty! There was a rocking-horse in the middle of the floor.

'Can I ride on it?' asked Mary Kate.

'Not today,' said Mummy. 'Wait till you come and stay here.'

A nurse in a pink uniform came out of a washroom.

'Haven't you any patients?' asked Granny.

'Not today,' said the nurse. 'They don't stay long in this ward, you know. We do sometimes have one left over till Tuesday, but we're nearly always empty on a Wednesday. We shall have some more tomorrow.'

She looked at Mary Kate and Teddy. 'Are you coming tomorrow?' she asked.

'No,' said Mary Kate. 'I'm coming the week after next.'

'I'll look out for you, then,' said the nurse.

'I like that pink nurse,' Mary Kate said as she followed Mummy and Granny back to the lift.

The week after next soon came. Mary Kate was up early on the Thursday morning. She came down the stairs before Daddy had finished his breakfast. He gave her a piece of toast.

'You needn't have got up yet,' he said. 'You don't have to go to the hospital till this afternoon, you know.'

'I've got a lot to do,' said Mary Kate. 'I have to put all my children to bed before I go. You will look after them, won't you, Daddy?'

'Of course,' promised Daddy.

In the middle of the morning Aunt Mary arrived. 'I couldn't let my one and only niece go into hospital without coming to make sure they gave her a comfortable bed,' she said, giving Mary Kate a little parcel.

Inside the parcel was a pair of red slippers with little golden bows on the toes. 'Granny sent them,' Aunt Mary said. 'I called to see her on my way here. She's coming to the bus stop to see us off.'

'Put the slippers in the basket with your dressing-gown,' Mummy said. 'Take your old ones out first, though. And don't forget to remind me to buy you a new toothbrush when we go out.'

Granny was already waiting at the bus stop when Mummy and Aunt Mary and Mary Kate came out of the churchyard. They had taken the short cut because Mary Kate wanted Aunt Mary to see the ducklings.

'They might not be there,' Mummy warned. 'They don't spend all their time by the bridge, you know.'

They were there, though. Mummy had brought some bread and Mary Kate dropped it over the rail into the stream. She gave Teddy to Aunt Mary to hold so that she wouldn't drop him, too.

'We *must* go now,' Mummy said, looking at her watch. 'We'll miss the bus if we don't.'

They hadn't been at the bus stop more than a minute or two when the bus came along.

'Toothbrush,' said Mary Kate, remembering.

'Too late now,' laughed Aunt Mary, helping Mary Kate on to the step.

'Can we go upstairs?' asked Mary Kate.

'Of course!' said Aunt Mary, so up they went.

'Good-bye, Granny,' shouted Mary Kate, looking out of the window and waving.

'Good-bye,' called Granny. 'See you on Saturday.'

There was no one else upstairs on the bus. Mary Kate and Teddy sat on one front seat and Mummy and Aunt Mary sat on the other. It was a long way to the hospital. After a little while Mary Kate went and sat on Mummy's lap and Teddy sat on Aunt Mary's lap and they all looked out of the wide window as the bus sped along the narrow lanes and through the quiet villages.

It was half past three when they reached the hospital. They had to go to Sister's office first and fill up a form.

'Where's Mr Smiley?' asked Mary Kate, when they came out.

'He'll come and see you presently,' Mummy told her.

A nurse in a blue uniform asked Mary Kate what her name was.

'Last bed on the right,' she said, when Mary Kate told her.

The ward seemed to be full of people. There were mothers and fathers and aunts and grand-mothers and children everywhere.

'There's the pink nurse,' Mary Kate said. She was holding Mummy's hand very tightly and feeling rather shy because of all the strangers in the room.

The nurse in the pink uniform smiled when she saw Mary Kate. 'Hallo,' she said. 'You've brought your Teddy, then. I hope he behaves himself.'

'Oh, he will,' promised Mary Kate. 'He's a very *good* bear!'

Mummy took Mary Kate's dressing-gown and slippers out of the basket and put them on the bed. Then she took out the sponge bag. 'Oh, dear!' she said. 'We forgot the new tooth-brush!'

'There might be a hospital shop,' Aunt Mary said. 'If not, there's a chemist just along the road. I remember seeing a blue glass jar in the window as we came by in the bus. Shall I go or will you?'

'I will,' said Mummy. 'I shan't be long.'

Off she went and Aunt Mary said, 'Come and have a ride on the rocking-horse, Mary Kate.'

While Mary Kate was having her ride the tea

trolley was wheeled in. Little tables were pulled into the middle of the room and in a few minutes all the children were sitting round them, eating sandwiches and cake and drinking mugs of milk or orange juice.

Mary Kate had an egg sandwich and a jam sandwich and a piece of sponge cake. Then the tea things were cleared away.

Mary Kate was playing with the doll's house in the toy corner when Mummy came back with her new toothbrush.

'Sorry I've been so long,' Mummy said. 'I had some tea.'

'So did I,' said Mary Kate.

'Good gracious!' cried Mummy. 'That was quick!'

'It was only a little tea,' Mary Kate told her. 'I wanted some more but they took it away.'

'Well, if nobody minds,' said Aunt Mary, 'I think *I'd* like to go and have a little tea.'

When Aunt Mary came back from having her tea Mummy and Mary Kate were nowhere to be seen.

'They're in the bathroom,' said the nurse in

the blue uniform, seeing Aunt Mary by Mary Kate's bed. Then Aunt Mary noticed that several of the children were in their dressing-gowns and slippers.

Mummy was just lifting Mary Kate into the big, deep hospital bath when Aunt Mary opened the bathroom door.

'Stand with your back to the door,' said Aunt Mary to Mummy. 'I've brought Mary Kate a lovely nutty cake.'

'She can't eat cake in *here*!' exclaimed Mummy. 'Whatever will the nurses say?'

'They won't know,' said Aunt Mary, taking a hazel nut cookie out of a paper bag. 'She can eat it in the bath. The crumbs will go down with the water.'

Aunt Mary broke off a piece of cookie and popped it into Mary Kate's mouth.

'Cake in the bath today and ice cream in bed tomorrow,' she said.

Mary Kate laughed. She thought Aunt Mary was joking. Nobody had ever given her ice cream in bed.

When she was bathed and dried Mummy put

her to bed. 'We must go now, darling,' she said.
'I'll come again tomorrow.'

As Aunt Mary kissed her she dropped a parcel
in Mary Kate's lap.

Mary Kate was so busy opening it she hardly
had time to wave to Mummy and Aunt Mary as
they went out of the door.

Inside the parcel was a paper bag and inside
the paper bag was another parcel in yellow
paper. Mary Kate pulled off the crepe paper and
there was a pair of red and white striped
pyjamas. They were just the right size for Teddy!

## Ice Cream in Bed

When Mary Kate woke up she was surprised to
see Daddy sitting by her bed.

'Hallo, Daddy,' she said. 'When did you
come?'

'Just this minute,' said Daddy. 'You were fast
asleep, so we waited for you to wake up.
Mummy's here, too.'

Mummy was sitting the other side of the bed,
by the window.

'How do you feel, darling?' she asked, smoothing Mary Kate's hair.

'All right,' said Mary Kate. 'My throat's sore.'

'We'll soon put that right,' said a cheerful
voice and there, at the bottom of the bed, stood
the pink nurse. She was holding a dish and a
spoon.

Mummy took the dish and showed it to Mary
Kate.

'Ice cream,' she said. 'Auntie said you'd be having ice cream in bed, didn't she?'

'Yes,' said Mary Kate, sitting up and reaching out her hand for the dish. 'Did you know Auntie gave me cake in the bath this afternoon, Daddy?'

'Did she?' laughed Daddy. 'Well, that's something *I've* never had! Come to think of it, I've never had ice cream in bed, either. It wasn't this afternoon you had the cake, though. It was yesterday.'

'Yesterday?' Mary Kate looked puzzled. 'I wasn't here yesterday.'

'Yes you were, pet,' Mummy told her. 'It's Friday today. Aunt Mary and I brought you here yesterday afternoon.'

'Friday?' said Mary Kate, slowly, spooning up her ice cream. 'Friday's the day Mr Smiley's going to make my nose better.'

'He's done it,' Daddy said. 'He did it this morning.'

Mary Kate put her hand up to her face to see if her nose was all right. It was.

'I don't remember,' she said in a puzzled voice.

Mummy smiled. 'You were asleep. We told you you wouldn't know anything about it, didn't we?'

'Was it magic?' asked Mary Kate, feeling her nose again.

'Sort of,' said Daddy. 'They give you something to make you sleep and when you wake up whatever has to be done has *been* done. I can't think of anything more magic than that, can you?'

'No,' agreed Mary Kate, finishing the ice cream. 'My throat has stopped being sore now. Shall I stop having ear-aches, too, when I come home?'

'I hope so,' said Mummy. 'And stop snoring and getting stuffy colds.' She took the dish away and put it on the locker. Teddy was lying there, in his new pyjamas. Mummy gave him to Mary Kate.

The pink nurse came back to collect the dirty dishes. All the other children had had ice cream, too. They were all sitting up in their beds, looking as sleepy as Mary Kate.

'Five more minutes,' said the nurse. 'We want to get them settled for the night.'

'What night?' asked Mary Kate.

'*This* night,' said Daddy. 'It's nearly bedtime.'

Mary Kate looked so bewildered that Mummy had to laugh. 'You've been asleep *all* day,' she said. 'Never mind, darling. You'll be coming home tomorrow.'

Mummy and Daddy kissed her 'Good-night' and turned to go. At the last minute Daddy took something out of his pocket and threw it on the bed. It was a little parcel.

'Another parcel?' said the pink nurse, coming to look. 'What is it this time, I wonder?'

She helped Mary Kate to unfasten the brown paper. Inside was a little doll, dressed like a nurse. Fixed to her arms by small rubber bands were two tiny baby dolls.

'Well!' exclaimed the pink nurse. 'Whatever will they think of next?'

She brought a bowl of warm water and took Mary Kate's sponge bag and hairbrush out of the locker.

'A little wash,' she said, 'and then I'll tidy your bed and you can go to sleep again. I expect you'll be going home tomorrow, won't you?'

'Yes,' said Mary Kate, shutting her eyes and holding up her face to be washed.

When Mummy and Daddy came to fetch Mary Kate the next morning they found her sitting up in bed, dressing Teddy.

'You're late,' she said. 'Some of the other children went straight after breakfast.'

'It's a long way to come,' Mummy said, taking Mary Kate's clothes out of her bag and putting the dressing-gown and slippers in.

When Mary Kate was dressed Daddy carried her out to the lift. Mummy followed them with the bag and Teddy. Mary Kate had put the little doll into Daddy's pocket so that the babies wouldn't catch cold.

'This isn't the way to the bus stop!' cried Mary Kate, as Daddy turned the corner outside the hospital.

'We're not going by bus,' said Daddy. 'We've got a surprise for you. Here we are.'

He stopped by a side street. A little way along the street was a small green car and standing by the car was Uncle Ned! Auntie Dot was looking out of the back window and waving her hand.

'We started out at the crack of dawn to come and visit you in hospital,' said Auntie Dot, when Mary Kate was safely settled on her lap and Mummy had climbed into the back seat beside them. 'We didn't know you would be coming home so soon.'

'I had the snuffle taken out of my nose,' Mary Kate told her. 'Mr Smiley did it with magic while I was asleep.'

'Lovely,' smiled Auntie Dot, cuddling Mary Kate up close. 'And you're quite better now, are you?'

'She's supposed to rest for a day or two,' Mummy said. 'She must go to bed when we get home and no rushing about for a little while.'

'I don't want to go to bed,' grumbled Mary Kate. 'I want to see Auntie Dot and Uncle Ned.'

'So you shall, poppet,' promised Auntie Dot. 'We'll come and sit by your bed and talk to you.'

She looked across at Mummy and smiled. Mummy smiled back. It was a special kind of smile. Mary Kate knew at once what it meant.

'More secrets,' she thought, happily. 'I wonder what it is this time?'

It wasn't long before she knew. As soon as Uncle Ned turned his little car into the drive Granny opened the front door.

'Everything's ready', she said. 'And lunch will be in about half an hour.'

'Good!' grinned Uncle Ned, rubbing his hands together. 'I'm rattling!'

Auntie Dot carried Mary Kate into the hall and through to the dining room Mummy came in with the bag. She warmed Mary Kate's pyjamas in front of the electric fire while Auntie Dot undressed her.

'Where's Auntie Mary?' asked Mary Kate.

'In her room, I expect,' said Mummy.

At that moment the door to the little room off the dining room opened and Aunt Mary came out. 'Ready?' she asked.

'Yes,' said Auntie Dot, fastening the last button on Mary Kate's pyjama jacket.

'Right, then,' said Aunt Mary and turned back into her room. Mummy picked Mary Kate up and followed Aunt Mary.

On top of Aunt Mary's bed was Mary Kate's blue eiderdown. Under the eiderdown was a big white bag.

'It's a sleeping bag,' Aunt Mary said. 'You put the pillow in the pocket at the top – see. Then you put yourself in the pocket at the bottom and we cover you up with the eiderdown. You can stay in bed down here in the daytime and we can take it in turns to come and talk to you. How's that?'

'Lovely,' sighed Mary Kate, snuggling down with Teddy. She was surprised to find that she really did feel rather tired.

'You have a little nap, pet,' Mummy said,

smoothing her hair. 'You can have your lunch when you wake up.'

Everyone had finished lunch by the time Mary Kate woke up. Daddy and Uncle Ned were chatting by the shed in the garden, Granny and Auntie Dot were looking at the flowers, Aunt Mary was drying the washing-up and Mummy was making a pot of tea.

'Mummy,' called Mary Kate. Mummy didn't come, but Jacky the dog did. He put his paws on the side of the bed and wagged his tail and tried to lick Mary Kate's face.

'Go and fetch Mummy,' said Mary Kate. 'Tell her I want my lunch.'

Jacky put his head on one side and barked. Mummy heard him and came to see what was the matter.

'I'm hungry,' said Mary Kate.

'I'll bring you some soup,' Mummy told her. 'And there's a little mashed potato and mince. All right?'

Mary Kate nodded. 'Back in a minute, then,' Mummy said but it wasn't Mummy who came back with the tray. It was Aunt Mary. She

brought her cup of tea in too, and drank it while
Mary Kate ate her lunch.

As Aunt Mary took the tray away Uncle Ned
appeared at the door. He was holding a glass
dish high above his head and over his arm was a
folded table napkin.

'Madam's dessert,' he said, bowing very low.
'They tell me that all the best people have their
ice cream in bed these days.'

# A Table for the Birds

It was Sunday morning. Mary Kate was already awake and playing with Og and Ben-Bun when Mummy went downstairs to make the tea. Mummy must have heard her talking to her toys, because when she came up with the tray she banged Mary Kate's door with her elbow and said, 'Come and have some tea, pet. I've brought your mug up.'

Mary Kate crawled carefully out of bed so as not to pull the blankets off Og and Ben-Bun and hurried out of her room and across the landing after Mummy.

There was a hump right in the middle of the big bed. It was Daddy. Only the top half of his face showed above the blankets and eiderdown. The pillows were pulled close round his head and his eyes were shut.

'Is Daddy asleep?' whispered Mary Kate,

climbing quietly into the bed.

Mummy smiled. She was arranging the cups on the tray. She pulled the little trolley table close up to the bed, kicked off her furry slippers and slid in beside Mary Kate.

'Move over, pet,' she said. 'Give Daddy a shake and make him wake up.'

Mary Kate shook Daddy's shoulder under the blankets but he wouldn't open his eyes. She tickled the back of his neck. He grunted and wriggled away. When she poked him in the back with her foot he put his hand behind him quickly and caught her ankle and held it fast.

Mary Kate giggled and squirmed herself over so that she could look at Daddy's face. His eyes were still shut but he was smiling. 'Wake up,' she said, 'or Mummy will drink your tea and I'll eat your biscuits.'

As soon as he heard this, Daddy let go of Mary Kate's ankle and sat up. He rubbed his eyes and yawned and pretended to be surprised to see her.

'Is it morning already?' he asked. 'I've only been asleep five minutes.'

Mummy sugared his tea and stirred it for him and Mary Kate kept very still while she handed him the cup and saucer. Then Mummy put the plate of biscuits on Mary Kate's lap and gave her her blue-and-white striped mug. It was only half full and not too hot so she drank the milky tea straight away and gave the mug to Mummy again.

Daddy helped himself to two biscuits but just as he was putting one in his mouth a bit broke off and dropped on to the floor.

'Oh, dear!' whispered Daddy to Mary Kate. 'Must pick that up before Mummy sees it.'

He drank his tea and held out the cup to Mummy, saying, 'More, please.' As soon as Mummy had turned away to pour the tea, Daddy leaned over the side of the bed and picked up the bit of biscuit. He hid it behind one of the pretty jars on the dressing-table. Mummy pretended not to know.

When they had all had two cups of tea and the biscuit plate was empty, they snuggled under the blankets for five minutes and then Mummy said it was time she got dressed and went down to start the breakfast.

Daddy was pretending to be asleep again, so Mary Kate wriggled up close to him and closed her eyes. After a few minutes she felt Daddy's big, warm hand fold round hers and give it a little squeeze.

'Don't make a sound, poppet,' he whispered in her ear. 'Just turn your head slowly and look towards the window.'

Mary Kate did as she was told. There, on the window-sill, sat a fat robin. The window was only open a little bit but the cheeky bird had found the way in without any fuss. Now he hopped down on to the dressing-table and stood

with his head on one side, listening.

Daddy and Mary Kate kept very still and watched him. He began to hop across the dressing-table, looking all about him. He pecked at Mummy's pretty rings on the little china tree and poked his beak into the blue dish that held her hairpins. Then he found the bit of biscuit that Daddy had hidden behind the jar of hand cream. He started to eat it, pecking bits off and gobbling them up very fast. Then, suddenly, he stopped eating, picked up the last bit of biscuit in his beak and flew out of the window with it.

'He's gone to give Mrs Robin her breakfast in bed,' said Daddy.

Mary Kate laughed. 'Won't Mummy be surprised when we tell her?' she said. 'She always puts crumbs on the kitchen window-sill for the birds' breakfast. Perhaps she hasn't put any out this morning.'

Mummy hadn't put any crumbs out. 'It's a waste of time,' she said. 'Pipkin eats them. And if he doesn't want them, he sits so close to the window that the birds won't come. What we need is a proper bird-table.'

'I thought we had one,' said Daddy, helping himself to toast.

'We did,' Mummy told him, 'but it's broken. The top fell off in the gales last winter. That's when I started putting the crumbs on the window-sill. We didn't have Pussy Pipkin then, though.'

'Oh, well,' Daddy said, reaching for his special marmalade, 'if the post is still there, all we need is a new table. A bit of wood nailed on to the post will do, won't it?'

'No, it won't,' Mummy said. 'It's got to be a tray so the food won't blow off and so high that Pipkin can't jump up on to it. That means putting in a new post – a tall one – well away from the trees and fences.'

After breakfast Daddy went out into the garden. He said he was going to look for a place to put the bird-table. He was gone a long time and when Mary Kate went out to look for him he wasn't there. She was just going back to the house when she heard someone whistling in the little wood at the bottom of the garden. It was Daddy. He came through the gate carrying a long, rough post over his shoulder.

'This ought to do,' he said, lowering the post to the ground. 'I'll just saw a bit off the crooked end and dig a hole for it.'

By the time the post was sawn and the hole dug, it was twelve o'clock. Mary Kate could hear the church clock striking. Daddy heard it, too. He stopped digging and looked at his watch.

'My goodness me!' he cried. 'Is that the time? I promised your Granny I'd take her some brussels sprouts this morning. If I don't get a move on she'll have to have them for tea instead of lunch. Run and fetch a basket, Mary Kate, while I plant this post.'

When Mary Kate came back with the basket Daddy was trying to hold the post steady with one hand and shovel the earth into the hole with the other. 'Hold the post,' he said. Mary Kate held it as best she could and Daddy filled in the hole and stamped the earth down.

'That'll have to do for now,' he said, wiping his hands on his trousers. 'Come and help me pick the sprouts. Granny's having visitors for lunch today.'

'Yes, she is,' said Mummy's voice behind them

and when Mary Kate and Daddy turned round they saw Mummy, with a colander in her hand. 'One o'clock lunch and you haven't even taken her the sprouts yet. You'll have to take her ours. They're all washed and ready for the pot. Put them in the basket and be off with you. I'll pick myself some more while you're gone. Have you finished the bird-table?'

'No,' said Daddy, tipping the clean sprouts into the basket. 'I've put the post in, though. It won't take long to make the tray.'

Mummy sniffed. 'Well, I hope you'll do it before the frosts come!' she said and hurried off to the vegetable plot.

Granny was very pleased to have the sprouts already washed.

'How thoughtful of you, dear,' she said. 'They're such fiddly things to do.'

Daddy looked at Mary Kate and Mary Kate looked at Daddy and they both looked at their feet and said nothing. They stayed talking to Granny and her visitors for so long that it was almost one o'clock before they started for home again.

'We're going to get into trouble for being late for lunch if we don't hurry,' Daddy said, as they went through the churchyard. 'As soon as we get into the field, you come up on my back and I'll run.'

Daddy ran all the way across the field and across the bridge and through the wood with Mary Kate bumping up and down on his back. Mummy was just taking the roast out of the oven when they arrived.

'Just in time,' panted Daddy, sliding Mary Kate on to the floor. 'I'll finish the bird-table after lunch.' He didn't, though. He went to sleep in his big chair by the fire. When he woke up it was almost tea-time.

'It's too dark to go outside and finish the bird-table now,' he said, peering out of the window at the low, grey sky.

'Just as well I finished it, then,' said Mummy, kneeling down in front of the glowing fire to toast the crumpets.

'*You* finished it?' cried Daddy, staring at her. 'This I must see!'

He went into the hall for his coat and then out

of the front door and round the side of the house to the garden. Mary Kate followed him, pulling her coat round her as she went.

Round by the vegetable plot they went and there was the thick post that Daddy had put in before lunch. There were four deep round holes in the soft earth close to the post and on top of it was a seed-box.

'She stood on a chair to nail it on,' Daddy said, looking into the seed-box. He lifted Mary Kate up and carried her back to the house. 'There's no doubt about it, Mary Kate,' he said. 'Your mother is a very remarkable woman!'

'Yes,' said Mary Kate. She didn't know what it meant but she thought it must be nice because Daddy was laughing.

# A Secret

Mary Kate had lost Mummy. It was silly, but she had. She stood on the top step of the house next door to Mrs Watson's wool shop and looked up the hill and down the hill, but Mummy wasn't there. Nor was Granny.

Mary Kate thought Granny had probably gone home, but she couldn't think what had happened to Mummy.

They had come out soon after lunch to do some shopping and bumped into Granny outside the Post Office. Granny said she was going to change her library book but she had one or two bits and pieces to buy so they all walked down the street together.

When they came to the Corner Store they saw that the windows had been decorated ready for Christmas. They looked so gay and pretty that they all stopped to have a good look.

The Corner Store was the biggest shop in the village. It had two doors and three windows and there was an upstairs to it, just like a town store.

Mary Kate liked the Corner Store. She liked to run up the red-and-black tiled path that was the left-hand entrance, go through the door and behind the middle window and come out of the other door on to the black-and-white tiled path that was the right-hand entrance. She could only do that in the summer, of course, because in the winter the shop doors were shut to keep the cold out. A bell rang when they were opened and the assistants looked up to see who was coming in. They wouldn't have been very pleased to see Mary Kate come in and go out again without buying anything.

'I want some tape,' Granny said and went in through the left-hand door. Mary Kate hopped in behind her before she could shut it and stop the bell ringing.

It was cosy inside the shop and a bit muddly. They sold so many things. There were groceries and sweets and bread and cakes and boots and shoes and curtain materials and dresses and coats and all kinds of interesting knick-knacks.

Then Mummy came into the shop. 'I've seen something in the window that I want,' she said. 'Upstairs.' She made a funny face at Granny. Granny stared at her and then said 'Oh – yes. Of course! Come on, Mary Kate, let's go and buy some chocolate drops.'

Mary Kate wanted to go upstairs with Mummy but she wanted some chocolate drops, too, so she went with Granny to the sweet counter.

Granny bought some sweets for herself while she was about it and then she saw a display of Christmas Gifts and went to have a closer look at it.

Mary Kate followed her but they were all gifts for grown-ups so she wandered away after a bit. She thought she would go upstairs and see what Mummy was buying. She had only taken two steps when Granny pulled her back.

'Come and help me change my library book,' she said. 'Mummy will catch us up when she's finished here.'

'What's she gone to get?' asked Mary Kate.

'Little girls shouldn't ask questions,' said

Granny. 'Not when it's nearly Christmas, anyway.'

She asked the assistant on the drapery counter to tell Mummy where she was going and then she and Mary Kate went out of the shop and round the corner and up the hill.

The pavement was so narrow Mary Kate had to walk behind Granny, holding on to her coat.

The library was at the back of Mrs Watson's Wool Shop. It was just a big bookcase all along the wall. There was a smaller bookcase in the corner, behind a pile of cardboard boxes and bundles of wool. This was where the children's books were kept.

Mary Kate went to see if her favourite book was there. It was about a little white kitten with a black patch over one eye and was full of lovely pictures.

Mummy came into the shop. She didn't come right down to the library. She said, 'Hallo' to Mrs Watson and then she called out to Granny, 'I'm going to the Bun Shop to collect my order.'

'All right, dear,' said Granny, without looking up. 'I shan't be long.'

Mary Kate was only halfway through the book about the White Kitten, so she didn't go after Mummy. She knew she would have to come back past the Wool Shop because that was the way they went home.

Two or three people came into the shop. Mary

Kate couldn't see the door from her corner behind the boxes but she heard the bell ring several times. Mrs Watson was having a busy afternoon.

Mary Kate came to the end of her book. She got up from the box she had been sitting on and went to find Granny. Granny wasn't there. There were three other ladies choosing books but Granny had chosen hers and gone away. She hadn't seen Mary Kate anywhere about so she thought she must have gone to the Bun Shop with Mummy.

Mary Kate went quickly out into the street. Mrs Watson didn't see her, so she didn't know she had been there all by herself. She didn't *hear* her go, either, because somebody opened the door to come in just as Mary Kate reached it and she went out without having to make the bell ring.

She couldn't see Mummy or Granny anywhere. Even when she climbed the five steps outside the house next to the shop she still couldn't see them.

She came down from the steps and went slowly

along the narrow path, down the hill to the Corner Store again. If she had gone *up* the hill she would have come, at last, to her own house, but she didn't think Mummy would go all the way home without her, so she went back to the village.

There was no one outside the Corner Store. The Bun Shop was on the other side of the road and there was rather a lot of traffic at the corner.

Mary Kate walked along the front of the Corner Store, past the newspaper shop towards the Post Office. She thought she would try to cross the road near the Church. It was quieter at that end of the village because there weren't any shops there.

When Mary Kate came to the corner opposite the Church she hesitated. This was the lane where Granny lived. She knew Mummy wouldn't be there but she thought Granny might, so she ran quickly down to Granny's cottage. Round to the back door she ran, and banged and shook at the handle. The door wouldn't open, so Mary Kate knew Granny wasn't home yet.

Mary Kate ran back to the end of the lane. A

bus was just coming up to the bus stop. She saw from the number on the front that this was the bus that would take her all the way home and put her down right opposite her own front door. There was a sixpence in her coat pocket. It had been there for ages because Mary Kate couldn't make up her mind what to do with it.

She put her hand into her pocket and felt the sixpence, but while she was wondering if the conductor would let her get on the bus by herself, he rang the bell and the bus moved off.

There was nothing coming either way so Mary Kate did her kerb drill very quickly and ran across. (She wasn't really certain which was left and which was right, so she looked both ways twice just to make sure.)

Down to the Bun Shop she ran, not stopping to look at anything on the way. Mummy wasn't there. The lady behind the counter knew Mary Kate but she didn't know she had lost Mummy. She thought Mummy was coming along behind somewhere.

She said, 'Hallo, Mary Kate. Tell Mummy her order's ready now.'

So Mummy's order hadn't been ready when she called for it. She would have to come back to the Bun Shop to collect it.

Mary Kate looked at the cakes and loaves in the Bun Shop window. They made her feel hungry. She remembered her sixpence. She was trying to make up her mind which cake she would buy when she noticed the shop next door.

It, too, had dressed its little bow window for Christmas. It was bright with tinsel and coloured paper and white with cotton-wool snow. In the middle of the bottom shelf was a Christmas crib. Mary Kate went to look at it.

Mummy came across the street from the hardware shop and Granny came round the corner from the Station Hill. A bus went by and a lady with a pram squeezed Mary Kate against the shop-front.

Granny and Mummy didn't see each other till they were both by the Bun Shop.

'Sorry I kept you waiting,' puffed Granny. 'I went to fetch my shoes from the menders. I met old Mrs Cotterill and she kept me talking.'

'That's all right,' Mummy said. 'My order

wasn't ready. I've had to come back for it.'

'Well, let's have tea in the Bun Shop, then,' Granny said. 'My treat.' She looked back at the little bow window of the toy-shop. 'Come on, Mary Kate. I'll buy you a doughnut,' she said.

Mary Kate followed Mummy and Granny into the warm, spicy-nice shop.

She fingered the sixpence in her pocket and smiled. She wouldn't have to buy a cake with it after all.

She sat down at the table and looked at Mummy and Granny. They were chattering and laughing just as though nothing had happened.

They didn't know they had lost her. Granny thought she had been with Mummy and Mummy thought she had been with Granny.

Mary Kate helped herself to a jammy dough-nut and bit a big sugary piece out of it. She had had an adventure and she was going to keep it a secret.

# A New Uncle

Uncle Jack was coming home. Granny had come bustling up the garden while Mummy and Daddy and Mary Kate were having breakfast, puffing and panting and waving a letter.

'Jack's in Paris!' she cried. 'He'll be here tomorrow.'

Mary Kate wanted to know who Jack was.

'Your other uncle,' Daddy told her. 'And don't talk with your mouth full.'

Mary Kate swallowed her cornflakes quickly and said she didn't remember Uncle Jack.

'You wouldn't,' said Daddy. 'He went off on his travels long before you were born.'

'He's been all round the world,' Granny said, proudly. 'Now he's coming home again.'

'Where does he live?' asked Mary Kate.

Daddy laughed. 'With Granny, of course,' he said. 'Where else?'

Then he stopped laughing and looked at Granny. So did Mummy.

'I know what you're thinking,' Granny said. 'He can't stay with me because I've turned the back bedroom into a bathroom. Well, he can have the attic. After all, it's where he and Ned slept when they were boys.'

'But it's full of junk!' cried Mummy.

'Yes,' said Granny. 'I came to ask you if you'd come and help me clear it out and spruce it up a bit.'

So Daddy and Mary Kate washed up while Granny and Mummy tidied and made the beds and then they all set off for Granny's house, taking Jacky the dog with them because they knew they would be away all day.

'What about lunch?' Mummy said as they came out of the churchyard into the village street.

'Soup and sandwiches,' said Daddy. 'This is an emergency.'

Granny went to send a telegram to Uncle Ned and telephone Aunt Mary while Mummy and Daddy and Mary Kate went to inspect the attic.

'Now don't get in the way, there's a good girl,' Mummy said as Mary Kate followed her up the narrow stairs. 'We've a lot to do.'

So Mary Kate tried to make herself small and keep clear of Mummy and Daddy as they carried odds and ends of furniture down into the garden.

Some of the smaller things they put on the first landing for Mary Kate to take down while they were in the attic moving something else. They said she was a great help and saved their legs a lot.

Granny came back with some paint and brushes.

'Charlie Bean's bringing the ceiling stuff for me,' she told them. 'And he's coming with his cart later on to take away all the things I want to get rid of.'

'Good,' said Daddy. 'This garden is looking more like Charlie's yard every minute.'

Charlie Bean was the rag and bone man. He had a junk yard near the station.

When he came with his horse and cart Daddy helped him to load up all the things Granny didn't want.

By this time the attic was almost empty. 'Now we can clean it up a bit,' said Mummy 'and then we'll have lunch and Daddy can whitewash the ceiling.'

Granny made the sandwiches and heated the soup while Mummy and Daddy swept and dusted in the attic to shift the worst of the dirt. Daddy had a duster tied over his head because he had forgotten to bring his garden cap. He looked like a pirate, Granny said.

In the middle of the afternoon Granny went out to do her Saturday shopping. She was going to do Mummy's too, because Mummy was helping Daddy do the ceiling.

Mary Kate didn't go with Granny. She stood by the attic door for a bit, watching Mummy and Daddy, and then she went down into the garden.

There was a man by the front gate. He was standing quite still looking at the house.

'Hallo,' he said. 'What's your name?'

'Mary Kate,' said Mary Kate. 'Granny isn't in. She's gone shopping.'

'She hasn't left you on your own, surely?' said the man.

'No,' said Mary Kate. 'Mummy and Daddy are here. They're whitewashing the ceiling.'

Just then Mummy came round the corner of the house to look for Mary Kate. She saw the man.

'Jack!' she cried and rushed down the path. The man put his arms round Mummy and lifted her right up in the air as though she had been a little girl.

'Put me down,' laughed Mummy. 'What are you doing here, anyway? You're not supposed to come until tomorrow.'

'Couldn't wait,' said the man who was Uncle Jack. 'So I flew.'

Mummy looked worried. 'It'll upset Mother,' she said. 'You know how she likes to have everything just so. She's doing up your room. It'll spoil it for her if you turn up before it's ready.'

'What do you want me to do, then?' asked Uncle Jack. 'Hide?'

'Yes,' said Mummy, making up her mind. 'You do just that. Mary Kate, will you take Uncle Jack back to our house and keep him there out of Granny's way?'

'Does she know the way?' asked Uncle Jack, doubtfully, looking at Mary Kate.

'Of course she does,' Mummy told him. 'She came across the fields all by herself once when I was stuck in the loft. Stop wasting time and get going before Mother comes back.'

Uncle Jack still looked doubtful. 'Won't she

wonder where the child is?' he asked.

Mummy had a bright idea. 'I'll fetch Jacky,' she said. 'I'll tell Mother she's taken the dog for a walk and she'll think they've gone up to the Green.'

The Green was a fenced-off field at the end of the lane. There were swings there and a see-saw. It was quite a safe place for Mary Kate to go on her own.

So Mary Kate set off with Jacky and Uncle Jack to take the short cut home. She felt very grown-up and important as she led the way through the churchyard.

Uncle Jack managed the stiff latch on the gate in the wall quite easily.

'It needs wiggling,' he said. 'It's wonky.'

'How did you know?' asked Mary Kate, surprised.

Uncle Jack laughed. 'I was wiggling this latch before you were born or thought of,' he told her. 'Which way now?'

'Down here,' said Mary Kate, leading him along the narrow alley between the hedge and the high brick wall. When they reached the

kissing-gate she stopped. 'You go first,' she said. 'Jacky always gets in a muddle with this gate.'

'Let him off the lead then,' said Uncle Jack. Then he went through the gate. 'Now you've got to pay me a forfeit,' he said.

'That's what Daddy says,' laughed Mary Kate and she gave her new uncle a kiss to make him open the gate.

Jacky was already a long way down the footpath that led to the bridge. Uncle Jack and Mary Kate hurried after him.

They stopped on the bridge to look at the stream. 'This is where we feed the ducks,' said Mary Kate. She was rather sorry the ducks weren't there for Uncle Jack to see.

'I know,' said Uncle Jack, throwing a pebble into the water. 'I used to come here when I was a boy, with your Uncle Ned. Aunt Mary too, and your mother.'

It seemed rather odd to Mary Kate to think of Uncle Jack and Uncle Ned and Mummy and Aunt Mary being children and feeding the ducks just as she did. She thought of them all in Granny's cottage – the two little girls in the back bedroom that was now the bathroom and the two boys in the attic. What a lot of room they must have taken up in Granny's kitchen.

Jacky was barking outside the back door by the time Uncle Jack and Mary Kate reached the gate at the bottom of the garden.

'So this is where you live, is it?' said Uncle Jack. 'Plenty of room for me, is there?'

'Oh, yes,' said Mary Kate. 'You can have Auntie Mary's room.'

She showed Uncle Jack where the tea-things

were and fetched the cake tin out of the larder because he said he was peckish.

By the time Mummy arrived Mary Kate and her new uncle were chatting and laughing as though they had known one another for years.

'I telephoned Mary,' Mummy said. 'She's coming down with Ned and Dot tomorrow. We're having a party.'

Uncle Jack went to Granny's house on Sunday morning as though he had just arrived and in the afternoon Mummy and Daddy and Mary Kate went across and pretended to be surprised to see him.

It was a *wonderful* party. Granny was so pleased to have all her family at home again.

Of course, when Uncle Jack had really settled in they told Granny how he had arrived a day too soon, but for quite a while only Mummy and Daddy and Aunt Mary knew how Mary Kate had taken her new uncle home and hidden him so that he wouldn't spoil Granny's surprise.

# The Wedding

It was the very middle of the night. Mary Kate was fast asleep with Teddy in his new pyjamas lying sideways on the pillow above her head. Mummy had put him there when she went to bed so he wouldn't sit on Mary Kate's face in the night.

Down in the dining-room the wall clock began to chime. Three o'clock, it said in its sweet, silvery voice but nobody heard it. Nobody was awake.

Upstairs on Mummy's bedside table the little alarm clock was busily ticking away the minutes. As soon as the dining-room clock stopped chiming, the whirring wake-up bell in the bedroom began to ring.

Mummy heard it and put out her hand to stop the noise. Daddy heard it and pulled the blankets over his head. Mary Kate didn't hear it. Her bedroom door was shut and so was Mummy's.

It was Mummy who woke Mary Kate, a little while later. She stood by the bed with a mug of milky tea in her hand, all dressed up to go out except for her coat.

'Wake up, pet,' she said. 'Drink up this tea and eat a biscuit or two and then I'll get you dressed.'

Mary Kate sat up and rubbed her eyes. 'Why have you got your hat on?' she said – and then she remembered.

This was the day Mummy's Cousin Ruth was getting married and Mary Kate was going to be a bridesmaid. Mummy had told her she would have to wake up before it was light because the wedding was going to be early and they had a long way to go.

When Mary Kate had had her tea and biscuits she went to the bathroom to wash. Daddy was there to help her so that Mummy wouldn't get her best dress splashed. Daddy was still in his dressing-gown. He said *he* only needed ten minutes to go from bed to bus stop.

'No use going to the bus stop this morning,' Mummy told him. 'The buses aren't running yet.'

It was just after four o'clock when they left the house. They closed the front door quietly and crept down the steps to the road. Daddy put the key through Mrs Next-Door's letterbox so that she could go in and look after Jacky and Pussy Pipkin when she woke up. It was very strange to be walking to the station in the dark, still, early morning. It wasn't a bit like being out late at night.

Here and there a street lamp shone softly but there were no lights to be seen anywhere in the silent houses. Not a car, not a bus, not a bicycle went by as they walked through the empty village. It seemed to Mary Kate that she and Mummy and Daddy were the only people awake in all the world.

Then they saw Granny and Uncle Jack. They came hurrying round the corner from the lane opposite the Church. Mummy and Daddy and Mary Kate stopped by the Post Office and waited for them.

'Thought we'd save you the trip to fetch us,'

Granny said as soon as she was near enough for them to hear her whisper. She took Mary Kate's hand and they all walked, whispering, to the station at the bottom of the hill.

The station was just as quiet and empty as the village. There was no one in the booking hall, no one in the waiting room and no one on the platform. The small yellow lights were a long way apart and not very bright. They made the dark places behind them seem darker still. It was so gloomy and different from the station in the daytime that Mary Kate had a funny feeling that it wasn't really her own village station at all.

A man in a peaked cap came out of an inner office and looked at them. He had a mug of tea in his hand and he was yawning. He opened the shutters on the booking office window and Daddy bought the tickets to London.

They heard the train coming long before they saw it. Then it swept round the curve of the line and into the station like a long, black caterpillar patterned all down its body with squares of yellow light.

There weren't many passengers on it and those that were sat huddled up in the corner seats, most of them half-asleep.

Mummy and Daddy and Granny and Uncle Jack settled themselves comfortably in corner seats and Mary Kate sat close to Granny and leaned her head against her.

'If I were you, Mary Kate,' Granny said, 'I should lie down on the seat and have a little nap. We don't want you falling asleep in the church, do we?'

Mary Kate didn't think she wanted a nap but she stretched herself out on the seat beside Granny and closed her eyes. Mummy took a cardigan out of one of the bags and covered her up with it.

The guard blew his whistle, the train began to move – and long before they reached the next station Mary Kate was asleep.

She slept all the way to London. Mummy had to shake her and rub her legs and lift her down on to the platform. Even then she didn't wake up properly. Daddy carried her across the big, busy station, through the brightly lighted ticket hall to the chilly yard, and they took a taxi to Auntie Dot's house.

It was nearly six o'clock and the grey morning light was making the street lamps look pale. Milk floats were rattling along the quiet streets and the sleepy houses were being woken up, their curtains drawn back, their bedroom windows opened.

Mary Kate was wide awake by the time they reached Auntie Dot's house. Uncle Ned opened the door to them and shouted 'They're here!' to Auntie Dot, who was in the kitchen.

'Right!' called Auntie Dot. 'I'll make the tea.'

'Good,' said Granny. 'That's what I like to hear,' and she and Mummy and Mary Kate took off their outdoor things and put them in Auntie Dot's front room. Daddy and Uncle Jack put their things on the hall-stand and went into the dining-room to warm their hands by the fire.

Mary Kate ate an *enormous* breakfast. When she finished her third piece of toast Auntie Dot said she'd better not have any more or her new dress wouldn't fit her.

'Am I going to put it on now?' asked Mary Kate.

'No,' said Mummy. 'We're all going to go upstairs and put on our wedding clothes now because we're only guests, but *you* don't change till you get to Cousin Ruth's house. You're special. You're a bridesmaid.'

Mummy and Granny had come up to London weeks ago to buy their wedding clothes. They had left them at Auntie Dot's house so they wouldn't get grubby and crumpled on the train journey. Aunt Mary had come down to the village to look after Mary Kate. She was going to be a bridesmaid, too. She had taken Mary Kate to the village church and told her exactly what was going to happen at Cousin Ruth's wedding.

When Mummy and Granny and Auntie Dot came downstairs again they looked very beautiful. They had pretty flowery hats on and they smelled lovely. Uncle Ned and Uncle Jack and Daddy looked rather splendid, too, in their striped trousers and tall hats.

At eight o'clock the hired car came to take them to Cousin Ruth's house. Though it was still so early in the morning, the house seemed to be full of people, all wearing new clothes.

Cousin Ruth was nowhere to be seen but Great-Aunt Jo came to the top of the stairs and called to Mary Kate to come up.

'In the back bedroom, darling,' she said, giving Mary Kate a little push. 'Dolly will see to you. I must finish dressing.'

There was a good deal of chatter and laughter coming from the back bedroom. Great-Aunt Jo opened the door and Mary Kate went in.

'Here she is!' said several people at once and then Aunt Mary was standing in front of her, looking like a princess in a long blue gown with pink roses at the hem.

There were eight bridesmaids altogether, three more tall ones in gowns just like Aunt Mary's and three more little girls wearing dresses like the one put out on the bed for Mary Kate. It was pink and frilly and all over ribbons and lace. Mary Kate thought it was lovely.

There seemed to be hands everywhere, un-buttoning her, pulling her skirt over her head, taking off her shoes and socks. Somebody wiped her hands and face with a warm wet sponge. It was the third time she had been washed that day – once at home and once at Auntie Dot's and now again at Cousin Ruth's!

Now she was being put into the pink frilly dress. Someone was straightening her new white socks and someone else was fastening one of her new white shoes. Cousin Ruth's sister, Dolly, began to brush Mary Kate's hair and then Aunt Mary fixed a little wreath of flowers on her head.

'There!' she said. 'Now we're all ready!' She

pushed Mary Kate towards the door, saying, 'Come and stand at the top of the stairs for a minute so Mummy can see you before she goes.'

'Where's she going?' asked Mary Kate in surprise.

'To the church,' Aunt Mary told her. 'The cars are here already. We'll be going ourselves in a minute or two.'

Mummy and Granny and Auntie Dot waved and smiled at Mary Kate as they went out of the front door. They were wearing flowers. Daddy and Uncle Ned and Uncle Jack had white carnations in their buttonholes.

There were four big shining cars in the road outside the house. They all had white ribbons on and looked very grand.

Soon it was Mary Kate's turn to go in one of the cars. She went with Aunt Mary and Cousin Dolly and one of the other little bridesmaids.

The church was full of people and flowers. The organ was playing softly and the morning sun shone through the tall windows in broken bits of colour. It was all so strange and beautiful that Mary Kate quite forgot to be nervous.

When the service was over, they all went outside and stood on the steps in the pale spring sunshine to have their pictures taken. Then, suddenly, it was raining confetti and rose petals and rice and everyone was laughing, and Cousin Ruth and the tall bridesmaids were squealing and running for the cars.

Uncle Ned lifted Mary Kate up so that she wouldn't be crushed.

'Where are we going now?' she asked.

'To the Royal Hotel for breakfast,' said Uncle Ned.

'We've *had* breakfast!' cried Mary Kate. 'We had it at *your* house.'

'This is the *wedding* breakfast,' Uncle Ned told her. 'There'll be a lot of it and it'll last a long time, so make the most of it, Mary Kate. It'll probably have to do us for lunch and tea as well!'

# Mary Kate and the School Bus

It was snowing. Mary Kate stood at the front window, watching the big flakes falling in the strange, unhurried way of snow beginning. Now they came straight down, now they turned and twisted and drifted sideways. The snow that fell on the road and on the front steps of the house melted at once. On the spiky plants of the rockery, though, the white flakes settled like sudden winter flowers.

A long, low green bus was coming up the hill. It was taking the older boys and girls from the village to the schools in the nearby town. At the same time a small blue bus was coming *down* the hill. It was the bus that collected the younger children from the country cottages and took them a roundabout way to the village school.

'I shall go on that bus when I go to school, shan't I, Mummy?' said Mary Kate. She had said it so many times before that Mummy didn't even bother to answer. All the same, she looked out to see the bus go by – and it was then she noticed it was snowing.

Mary Kate had said it was, but Mummy hadn't been listening.

'What a nuisance!' cried Mummy. 'I hope it's not going to last. We had enough of it at Christmas. I thought we'd finished with snow for this winter.'

She flicked her duster rather crossly round the room and then went upstairs to make the beds.

Mary Kate pressed her nose against the cold window-pane. She had been hoping the snow *would* last because she wanted Daddy to help her make a snowman. They had made a lovely one at Christmas.

The snow was falling faster now. There was a scattering of white flakes on the front steps and the rockery was all over snow-flowers.

By lunchtime the snow was quite thick but the steps were clear. Mummy had swept them. She banged the broom hard against the wall to show how annoyed she was.

'We *must* go to Granny's,' she said. 'I promised to do some shopping for her this afternoon. She's got such a nasty chesty cough she can't possibly go out.'

Mary Kate was delighted to hear they were going out in the snow but she put on a worried face and said 'Oh, dear!' because she could see Mummy didn't want to go.

After lunch Mummy dressed Mary Kate in her warm trousers over her skirt and her long boots over her trousers. She had to wear two pairs of socks because the boots were a bit too big.

Mummy pulled Mary Kate's hat well down over her ears, wound her scarf twice round her neck and tucked the tops of her mittens into the sleeves of her coat.

'There,' she said. 'You'll do.'

Mary Kate didn't feel as though she would do at all. She felt so bundled up she didn't think she could move. She could, though. She plodded down the front steps holding Mummy's hand, which she couldn't feel because of her thick mittens and Mummy's furry gloves.

When they reached the front gate they saw

that no one had walked along the narrow foot-path since the snow started that morning. The snow was clean and beautiful, just waiting for Mary Kate to mark it.

She put her feet down slowly and carefully, watching her big boots sink deep into the snow. She thought she was walking straight but when she looked over her shoulder she saw her foot-prints following her all wiggly. Mummy's foot-prints were wiggly, too, and rather smudgy. She wasn't walking as carefully as Mary Kate.

They caught the bus to the village. It had stopped snowing while they were having lunch but by the time they got off the bus it had started again.

'I hope this doesn't keep on all afternoon,' Mummy said, but it did.

By three o'clock the snow was really deep. It looked so chilly outside that even Mary Kate didn't want to leave Granny's cosy little parlour and set out for home.

'I meant to catch the ten to four bus,' said Mummy, anxiously watching the fast falling snow. 'I wonder how long we shall have to

wait for it? It's sure to be running late.'

'Why don't you go up early and get a lift on the school bus?' suggested Granny. 'Mr Beadle is very obliging. He doesn't mind giving the mothers a lift when they come to meet the children in bad weather.'

'I think we will,' Mummy said. 'After all, he passes the door. Get your things, Mary Kate. We'll warm them by the fire so you can start out nice and comfortable.'

Mr Beadle didn't in the least mind giving

Mummy and Mary Kate a lift in his little blue bus. There was plenty of room. Mary Kate thought it was lovely to be on the school bus at last but she was glad Mummy was with her. She didn't really know any of the children even though some of them waved to her whenever they saw her standing in the window or at the front gate, waiting for the bus to go by.

The bus climbed slowly up the hill towards Mary Kate's house. A huge lorry, with a long trailer loaded with wood, was coming down the hill. Suddenly the lorry skidded, swung sideways across the road and stopped with its front stuck in the hedge. The trailer swung round, too, and the tail of it crashed through the hedge on the other side of the road.

All the children cried out when they saw the lorry skid. Mr Beadle pulled the bus well over to the side of the road and stopped. Then he climbed out and went, as fast as he could, up the hill towards the lorry, but before he reached it the lorry driver was out on the road, wiping his forehead with his handkerchief and looking at the mess.

'Thank goodness the driver wasn't hurt,' Mummy said, when she saw he was all right. 'And thank goodness it didn't happen a few yards higher up. He'd have crashed into our front garden.'

The next few moments were busy ones. Several cars and vans came up the hill behind Mr Beadle's bus. They had to stop, of course. One of them drove across to the other side of the road, reversed in a gateway and went back to the village. Then Mr Turner, the policeman, arrived on his scooter and Mr Beadle came back to the bus and said the breakdown truck had been sent for but he didn't know how long it would be.

'It looks as if we're in for a long wait,' Mummy said. 'And we're so near home, too. I wonder if we could get by? Come on, Mary Kate, let's try.'

So Mummy and Mary Kate got out of the bus and went up the hill to where the lorry was.

It was no use. They saw that they couldn't possibly squeeze themselves between the lorry and the hedge. Nor could they get between the lorry and the trailer, even if they ducked down low.

The long, low green bus appeared on the other side of the lorry. Here was another load of school children who were going to be late for their teas.

The driver of the green bus came to talk to the lorry driver. So did Mr Beadle. They said that if the lorry driver could move back just a little bit the children could change over buses.

'I can take my lot home in Mr Beadle's bus and he can take his lot in mine,' said the driver of the green bus.

'Sorry, mate,' the lorry driver said. 'I can't shift her. I've tried. She's wedged right up against the trailer and the wheels just spin round in this snow.'

He looked at Mummy and Mary Kate, who were standing there shivering and wondering if they could get into their back garden by way of the field. They were so near, it seemed silly not to be able to get into the house.

'You and the kiddy had best get up in my cab, lady,' said the lorry driver. 'You'll freeze out here.'

Mary Kate felt that her feet were freezing already, in spite of the two pairs of socks. She was very glad indeed to be lifted up into the high cab of the lorry, out of the way of the wind and the stinging snow.

She and Mummy had hardly settled themselves in the seats when Mummy gave a funny little screech.

'What an idiot I am!' she cried. 'All we have to do is get down the other side.'

She leaned across Mary Kate and opened the door. Mary Kate made herself small while Mummy squeezed past her and in another moment she was being lifted out of the lorry and put down on the footpath outside her own front gate.

'Thanks very much,' called Mummy to the lorry driver.

The lorry driver stared at the empty cab. So did the driver of the green bus. Then they started to laugh.

'Thanks, lady,' shouted the driver of the green bus as Mummy put her key into the front door. 'You must think we're a bright lot.'

Mummy and Mary Kate couldn't imagine what he meant but it wasn't long before they knew.

They stood in the front window watching the children from the green bus climb through the cab of the lorry and straggle down the hill towards Mr Beadle's bus. Then little children from Mr Beadle's bus came up the hill and were lifted through the cab and helped into the green bus. In a little while both buses had been turned round and all the children were on their way home. Some of the big boys and girls were walking because Mr Beadle's bus was too small to take them all.

It was dark before the lorry and trailer were set straight on the road again. It took a long time to do, and a lot of tea and a great plate of sandwiches went out to the lorry driver before it was done. Mary Kate watched it all, eating her tea at the little table in the window.

She was sorry when the lorry driver waved good-bye to her and drove away. She had been half hoping Daddy would have to climb through the cab when he came up the hill from the station.

# Mary Kate Goes to School

Mary Kate was five. She had been five for a whole week and tomorrow she would be going to school.

'You must have your hair washed this morning,' Mummy said, while they were having breakfast.

Mary Kate put on a scowly face. She didn't like having her hair washed.

Mummy pretended not to see the scowl. 'Granny said she might look in this afternoon,' she said.

Mary Kate brightened up a bit. 'I hope she does,' she said. 'Then I can show her all my school things.'

Mummy had put all Mary Kate's school things on the little blue dressing-table in her bedroom, ready for the morning. Mary Kate went upstairs straight after breakfast to have another look at them.

First she looked at her new sandals. Her old ones didn't fit her any more. They had gone to a jumble sale. Next to the sandals was a pair of brown strap shoes. Mary Kate could do them up all by herself. She couldn't tie shoelaces properly yet. She tied them all loose and tangly so that her shoes fell off when she hurried or the laces came undone and tripped her up.

Next to the shoes was a pair of black plimsolls. Mary Kate had never had plimsolls before because she had never needed them. She picked them up and sniffed at their strange, rubbery smell. Then she stretched the elastic front of one of them, to see it spring back into shape.

Mummy had been to several shops to find the elastic-fronted plimsolls. 'You'll be a nuisance to your teacher if you have lace-up ones,' she had said.

That was really how Mary Kate had come by the strap shoes. 'Shan't I be a nuisance with my shoes?' she had asked, looking down at her brown lace-ups.

So Mummy bought her new shoes and Granny bought her three pairs of short white socks. When they arrived home with all the shoes and socks, they found a parcel in the back porch. It was from Aunt Mary and inside it was a school satchel.

'This is to carry all your bits and pieces to school,' said the card that was with the satchel.

'What bits and pieces?' asked Mary Kate.

'All sorts of things,' Mummy told her. 'You'll see.'

One of the bits and pieces arrived the very next day. It came from Auntie Dot and Uncle Ned. It was a bright red pencil case. Inside it was a little ruler, a rainbow-coloured pencil with a rubber on the end, a blue pencil without a rubber and a rubber without a pencil.

'You'll need a pencil sharpener,' Daddy said, when he saw the pencil case, so he bought her one.

Mary Kate was very pleased. She had never had so many new things before, except at Christmas or on her birthday.

Now all the things were on her dressing-table and tomorrow she would put on her brown pleated skirt and a shirt blouse and wear her new white socks and her strap shoes. She touched the toe of the left shoe with the tip of her finger and then rubbed the place quickly with her handkerchief so as not to leave a mark on the shiny brown leather.

When Granny came that afternoon, she brought two more surprises for Mary Kate. The first was a box of coloured pencils from Uncle Jack and the second was a painting pinny, which Granny had made.

It was green with a pattern of tiny squares and squiggles all over it. 'I thought it was just the right sort of pattern for a painting pinny,' Granny said. 'A few more spots and splashes will hardly show. And it doesn't matter which way round you wear it because it's just one long piece of stuff with a hole in the middle for your head. The girdle is sewn on quite firmly, all you have to do is tie it round your waist.'

She slipped the pinny over Mary Kate's head, to see if it fitted her. It did.

Mary Kate pulled the pinny off again, rumpling her newly-washed hair. As she gave it

to Granny to fold she caught sight of a strip of
white tape with writing on it.

'What does that say?' she asked, turning the
pinny round to look.

'It says Mary Williams,' Granny told her. She
looked across at Mummy. 'Haven't you taught
the child to recognize her own name yet?' she
asked.

'Of course I have,' Mummy said, 'but not like
that.' She took her shopping pad and pencil

from the kitchen cabinet. 'Write your name for Granny,' she said.

So Mary Kate sat down at the table and wrote her name. She wrote it slowly and carefully in big, round, wobbly letters – Mary Kate Williams. The e and the s were back to front, but it was quite easy to read.

'That's very good,' nodded Granny, when she saw it. 'I'm sorry I didn't put Kate on your pinny. Never mind, you'll know it's yours, won't you?'

The next morning Mary Kate was down in the dining-room before Daddy had even started his breakfast.

'My word, you're early this morning,' he said.

'I'm going to school today,' said Mary Kate.

'So you are!' cried Daddy, pretending he had forgotten. 'Well, you'd better come and eat a hearty breakfast. You'll need to keep your strength up. Here, have one of my eggs.'

So Mary Kate had one of Daddy's boiled eggs and Mummy put another one in the saucepan for him and an extra one in case Mary Kate felt like eating two.

'Bread and butter?' asked Daddy, cutting a slice into fingers. He called them soldiers. He said the little crusty one at the end was the sergeant.

As soon as Daddy had gone, Mummy and Mary Kate went upstairs to get dressed.

Mary Kate fastened her shoes herself, just to show Mummy that she could. When she was dressed, she looked very smart – except for her hair, which was all night-wild and anyhow.

Mummy brushed out the tangles and tied the hair back with a ribbon.

'There!' said Mummy. 'You'll do.'

Mary Kate looked at herself in the mirror and thought she didn't look like Mary Kate at all. It was very odd. She didn't even *feel* like Mary Kate this morning.

'Are we going on the school bus?' she asked, as Mummy helped her into her coat.

'Not this morning,' Mummy said. 'We'll walk across the field. We've plenty of time. We'll get there nice and early, so you can find your way about a bit before school starts.'

So they went out the back way. Mummy had

to push Jacky back into the kitchen and shut the door quickly, because he wanted to go with them. They could hear him barking as they went down the garden and through the gate into the wood. There were primroses growing by the path. Mary Kate would have liked to pick some but Mummy told her not to stop today.

So she hurried after Mummy along the path to the stile and across the field to the little bridge. There they stopped for a moment, because the ducks were coming.

'No bread today, ducks,' called Mary Kate. 'I'm going to school.'

The ducks took no notice of her. They just swam under the bridge and away round the bend in the stream.

Mummy and Mary Kate went on across the field. When they came to the kissing-gate, Mary Kate ran through first and held the gate shut.

'Pay me! Pay me!' she cried, so Mummy paid her a kiss to make her open the gate.

The weedy footpath behind the churchyard was too narrow for them to walk along side by side, so Mary Kate trotted along behind, taking care not to tread on Mummy's heels. Mummy wiggled the latch of the gate in the churchyard wall and they went through the churchyard and out into the village street.

There was the school, a little way beyond the church – and there were the school children, in ones and twos, dawdling into the playground.

Mary Kate began to feel a bit funny inside. She held Mummy's hand now, very tightly.

Mummy looked across the road towards the little lane where Granny lived.

'Good gracious me,' she cried. 'There's Granny, standing at her gate. Look, she's seen us. She's waving. Wave to her, Mary Kate.'

So Mary Kate waved to Granny. She jumped up and down and waved so hard that her satchel bumped about and banged her on the back.

'Let's go and have a quick word with her,' suggested Mummy. 'We've got time.'

'My goodness, Mary Kate,' said Granny, when they reached her cottage. 'You *do* look smart. And so grown-up.' She put her hand into her pocket and pulled out a little packet.

'Here's something else to put in your satchel,'

she said. 'Biscuits. In case you feel peckish when you have your mid-morning milk.'

'Thank you,' said Mary Kate. She swung her satchel round to the front and unbuckled it and put the biscuits inside. Mummy had already told her about the mid-morning milk. She was looking forward to having a little bottle all to herself and a straw to drink through.

They said good-bye to Granny and Mary Kate went off down the lane a little way ahead of Mummy, feeling quite happy. She turned and waved to Granny just once more before she and Mummy crossed the road. Then she let go Mummy's hand and skipped along the path towards the open gate of the playground, just as Uncle Jack and Uncle Ned, Auntie Mary and Mummy had done, when they were children.

# A Name and an Elephant

Mary Kate was following Mummy and Mummy was following Miss Chesney. Miss Chesney was the Headmistress. Mummy and Mary Kate had been in her office answering questions while she filled in a form. Now she was taking them to see Mary Kate's classroom and meet her teacher.

The classroom had big windows, set high in the wall. Through one of them Mary Kate could see the top of a tree and a patch of sky and through the other she could see the church tower. All round the walls were paintings and drawings and big coloured diagrams and pictures. In one corner was a doll's house and a cot with a doll in it and in another corner was a table piled with books. There was a stove with a huge fireguard round it and, most wonderful of all, there was a little playhouse, with windows and a door and real curtains. Mary Kate wanted to run across the room and peep inside it but Miss Chesney was speaking to someone who had just come in.

'Ah, there you are, Miss Laurie,' she was saying. 'We have a new pupil this morning.' She put her hand on Mary Kate's shoulder. 'This is Mary Kate,' she said, 'and this is her mother. Mrs Williams, this is Miss Laurie. She will be Mary Kate's teacher.'

'How do you do,' said Mummy and Miss Laurie together, and then Miss Laurie said, 'Hallo, Mary Kate. I'm so glad you've come to join us. The others will be in soon. Would you like to have a quick look round before they come, then I'll show you where to put your coat.'

Off went Mary Kate, to look in the playhouse. Inside were two tiny chairs and a little table, a small set of shelves on a box, painted to look like a dresser, and a bushel box on end, painted to look like a cooker. On the dresser were dolly pots and pans and cups and saucers and plates.

Mary Kate just stood there, looking and looking and thinking what marvellous games she could have in the little house, with Teddy and Black Bobo and Dorabella and Og, the

Golly. Then she remembered that they were all at home, still tucked in their beds, while she was at school.

'Mary Kate,' said Miss Laurie's voice. The door of the little house opened and the teacher looked in. 'Mummy's going now,' she said. 'Come and say good-bye to her and I'll show you where to put your things.'

Mary Kate followed Miss Laurie and Mummy out of the classroom into the cloakroom. There were pegs low down all round the wall and two little low-down washbasins. Everything was just the right height for Mary Kate.

'Good-bye, pet,' Mummy said, giving her a quick kiss. 'I'll come and fetch you after school.'

'This will be your peg,' said Miss Laurie, almost before Mary Kate had time to say good-bye to Mummy. 'Let me help you with your coat.'

Mary Kate looked at the peg. It had a picture of a red elephant just above it.

'Do you know what this picture is?' asked Miss Laurie, hanging Mary Kate's coat on the peg and putting her hat on top.

'Elephant,' said Mary Kate and then she saw that all the pegs had pictures and they were all different. The other pegs had names, too, but Mary Kate's didn't.

'Good,' smiled Miss Laurie. 'Now you just remember that your hat and coat are hanging under the red elephant and you won't lose them. I'll print out a name for you in a moment, but I'll find you a place in the classroom, first.'

She showed Mary Kate a little table and chair. 'You can sit here,' she said. 'There's a drawer to put your things in and this is so you won't forget where you are.'

She took a card out of a box and fixed it firmly to a corner of the table with four big drawing pins. It was a picture of a red elephant, just like the one in the cloakroom.

'Now I'll just get a card for your name,' said Miss Laurie, looking in another box. 'Then I'll go and ring the bell and let the others in. Now, what shall I put on this card? What do they call you at home?'

'Mary Kate,' said Mary Kate, surprised, wondering what else they could call her.

'Right,' said Miss Laurie. 'That's what we'll call you, then. That way we shan't muddle you up with the other Mary.'

Mary Kate said nothing. She wasn't sure she liked the idea of another Mary.

Miss Laurie went out of the room and a moment later Mary Kate heard the clanging of a bell close by. The noise was so loud she had to put her hands over her ears to shut it out.

Then the children came in, talking and laughing and pushing at one another, struggling to hang up their hats and coats. Mary Kate could see them through the open door of the classroom. There seemed to be a great many of them. She hoped they weren't *all* coming in, but they were.

They clattered into the classroom and made their way to their places, all staring at Mary Kate as they passed her. Some carried satchels, some carried books and some had dolls and teddy bears.

Mary Kate wished she had brought her Teddy to school with her – or even Og, the Golly.

A little girl with a long, fair pigtail came and stood next to Mary Kate. Mary Kate had a feeling she had seen her before, somewhere, but she couldn't think where.

'You've come, then,' said the little girl. 'What's your name?'

Mary Kate told her.

'I'm Susan,' said the little girl. 'Susan Bates.' She nodded towards another little girl with untidy dark hair falling about her face. 'That's Jane. She lives next door to me.'

Then Mary Kate knew where she had seen Susan before. She and Jane were two of the children who travelled on the school bus. They had often waved to Mary Kate as she stood at the front gate.

A boy in a green jersey came and stood by Susan. 'Who's she?' he asked, nodding towards Mary Kate.

'Mary Kate,' said Susan. 'She's new.'

Mary Kate felt very new indeed as she watched the children go to their places and show one another the things they had brought to school. Then Miss Laurie rapped on her desk for silence and began to call the register.

When Miss Laurie said 'Mary Turner,' Mary

Kate stared at the little girl who answered. She had short fair hair, held back with a blue Alice band. Mary Kate didn't think she looked in the least bit like another Mary.

She was so busy thinking about it that she didn't hear Miss Laurie call her name. Susan had to nudge her, to make her answer.

'You're the last one,' said Susan. 'Valerie Watson used to be last, but now you are.'

Mary Kate liked being the last name on the register. It made her feel special.

'Susan,' called Miss Laurie, 'show Mary Kate the doll's house and all the other things. Perhaps you'd like to play house with her, for a while.'

So Susan took the doll out of its cot and Mary Kate dressed it and sat it on a chair in the little house, and they played a marvellous game, with Mary Kate being mother and Susan being father and the milkman and the baker and the district nurse, who had to come because the doll baby was ill.

In the middle of the morning all the children had a little bottle of milk, just as Mummy said they would. Mary Kate bent her straw and Miss

Laurie gave her another one. Susan helped her
eat the biscuits Granny had given her and then
they both went out into the playground to run
about till the bell went.

After playtime, Miss Laurie gave Mary Kate
some wax crayons and a huge sheet of paper
and told her to draw a picture to take home to
Mummy. She drew the playhouse.

When the bell rang again, Mary Kate thought it must be time to go home, but Susan said it wasn't.

'We haven't had our dinner yet,' she said. 'Don't you want any?'

Mary Kate *did* want her dinner. She ate it all and then she had two helpings of apricots and rice. Afterwards, Susan tried to teach her to skip but Mary Kate kept tripping over the rope, so they played 'higher and higher' with some of the other children.

In the afternoon Miss Laurie read a story to the class, but Mary Kate didn't hear much of it. She was fast asleep on the floor by the doll's house.

When she woke up the children were singing.

'This old man,' they yelled, 'He played one . . .'

Mary Kate knew that song because Granny sang it to her, so she joined in and yelled with the others.

Then it really *was* time to go home. Mary Kate rushed into the cloakroom with Susan and there was Mummy, standing by the door.

Mary Kate ran to her and hugged her. 'I drew

you a picture,' she said, 'and I cut a blue cat out of sticky paper and I went in the playhouse and I played with the doll and I had two puddings and Susan taught me how to play "higher and higher". That's Susan, over there, with the long hair. She's my best friend. She says I can sit next to her on the school bus tomorrow. Can I, Mummy?'

'We'll see,' smiled Mummy. 'Which is your peg?'

'The one with the elephant,' Mary Kate told her, but when she looked at the elephant she saw that Miss Laurie had put a card with her name on above it.

Mary Kate Williams, she had written, in big, round, red writing.

'That's right,' said Mary Kate, touching the card with her fingertips. 'That's my name. Mummy, did you know there's another Mary? She's in my class . . .'

'Is she?' said Mummy, picking Mary Kate's hat up from the floor. 'Never mind. There's only one Mary Kate.'

Mary Kate buttoned her coat up crooked.

'Tomorrow I'm going to be father,' she said, 'and Susan's going to be mother. And I'm going to stick my blue cat in a book and write "cat". Susan said I could.'

# The Fairy Tooth

Mary Kate had a loose tooth. When she put her tongue behind it, it moved. It was one of her four front teeth so she stood in front of the mirror and pushed at the tooth to see if she could see it moving. She couldn't. It wasn't loose enough for that.

'My tooth moves,' she said, when she went downstairs to breakfast.

'Oh, no!' cried Mummy. 'Let me see.'

'You can't see it,' Mary Kate told her. She made a toothy face at Mummy. 'I can feel it, though. I can move it with my tongue.'

Mummy gave a big sigh. 'Oh, dear, what a pity. I suppose it had to come, but I did hope you wouldn't start losing your teeth just yet.'

Mary Kate was puzzled. 'I haven't lost it,' she said, feeling the tooth with her fingertip, to make sure. 'It's still there.'

'Not for long,' Mummy said. 'They'll all come out, sooner or later. They're your baby teeth. In a few years they'll all be gone and you'll have your grown-up teeth.'

Mary Kate didn't say anything. She was too busy trying to bite a piece of toast without using her loose tooth. A day or two later, Mummy said, 'How would you like to have lunch and tea with Granny on Saturday?'

'Why?' asked Mary Kate.

'Because Daddy and I want to go into town and do some shopping,' Mummy said.

Mary Kate wanted to know what sort of shopping. Sometimes she liked going shopping and sometimes she didn't.

'Clothes, mostly,' Mummy told her. 'Daddy wants some shirts and socks. And I'd like some summer shoes and at least one cotton dress. We'd like to have a good look round. Granny thought you'd rather stay with her.'

Mary Kate thought so, too. Shirts and socks and shoes were the sort of shopping she didn't like.

'Will Uncle Jack be there?' asked Mary Kate,

when she and Mummy and Jacky, the dog, were on their way to Granny's on Saturday morning.

Mary Kate hadn't known her Uncle Jack very long. He had been travelling round the world ever since she was born and had only come home a few months ago. He still travelled a lot, but not very far now, so he stayed with Granny most week-ends.

'I'm not sure if he'll be home this week or not,' Mummy said. 'Granny didn't say.'

'I hope he is,' Mary Kate said, skipping along the narrow path behind the churchyard. She liked Uncle Jack. He told her marvellous stories about his adventures abroad.

When they reached Granny's cottage, they saw that Uncle Jack *was* there. He was in the yard, chopping firewood. Jacky rushed at him and nearly knocked him over. He liked Uncle Jack, too.

'Hey!' cried Uncle Jack. 'Call off your horrible hound. He's eating me. Why don't you feed him before you bring him out?'

'Down, Jacky,' Mummy said, jerking at the lead.

'*Jacky!*' snorted Uncle Jack. 'Whatever made you call him that?'

'He reminded me of you,' said Mummy. 'He never stayed put for more than five minutes at a time.'

Uncle Jack threw a piece of kindling at her. Mummy ducked and the stick hit the dustbin. Jacky leapt after it, thinking it had been thrown for him to chase. He crashed into the bin and the lid fell off, with a terrible clatter.

Granny poked her head out of the bathroom window.

'What's all that noise?' she called, but nobody told her. They were all laughing too much to speak.

Mummy gave Mary Kate a bag with her brush and comb and pinafore in it. Then she went home.

'I've a bit of shopping I must do this morning,' Granny said, when she had made the beds. 'I wonder if I can trust you and Uncle Jack to keep an eye on the lunch for me?'

'No, you can't,' Uncle Jack said, coming in from the yard just in time to hear her. 'But you can trust us to do the shopping. You'll come with me, won't you, Mary Kate?'

'Yes,' said Mary Kate at once. This was going to be the kind of shopping she *did* like.

Granny made out a list of the things she wanted and gave Mary Kate a basket to carry.

'May I buy myself a jammy doughnut for my tea?' asked Uncle Jack, as they went out of the front door.

'Yes,' said Granny, 'and you may buy one for Mary Kate, too.'

189

Mary Kate trotted happily along beside Uncle Jack, carrying the empty basket. First they went to the Post Office to buy a book of stamps and then they went to the greengrocer's for the fruit and vegetables that Granny wanted.

'Let's buy Granny some flowers,' suggested Uncle Jack. 'What do you think she'd like? Daffodils or anemones?'

'Both,' said Mary Kate, so they bought both.

Uncle Jack put the flowers carefully on top of the basket. 'I'd better carry it now,' he said. 'It's heavy.'

They crossed the road to the Bun Shop and Uncle Jack looked at Granny's list. 'Malt loaf,' he said, 'and a large wholemeal.'

'Don't forget the jammy doughnuts,' Mary Kate reminded him.

'Now we'll go to the Tuck Shop,' said Uncle Jack, when they had bought the bread and cakes. 'I fancy some peanut crunch. How about you?'

'I don't think I can eat it,' Mary Kate told him. 'I've got a loose tooth. It wobbles when I bite something hard.'

'Oh, bad luck,' said Uncle Jack. He bought

her some chocolate drops and jelly fruits and then he bought a box of crystallized ginger for Granny.

'That's the lot,' he said, checking with the list. 'Home now.'

Lunch was ready by the time they arrived.

Mary Kate helped Granny to set the table while Uncle Jack carved the joint.

There was apple pie and custard for pudding. Mary Kate was half-way through hers when she suddenly made a gurgly noise and put her hand to her mouth.

'There's a hard thing in my pie,' she said. 'It must be a stone.'

She took the hard thing out of her mouth.

'Apples don't have stones,' Granny said. 'Whatever can it be?' She leaned over to have a look.

'Why, it's your tooth!' she cried, when she saw what was in Mary Kate's hand.

'I never knew my tooth looked like that!' said Mary Kate, staring at the tiny, shiny thing.

She put her tongue into the place where the tooth had been. 'How did such a little tooth come out of such a big space?' she asked, wonderingly.

'It isn't really a big space,' Granny told her. 'It just feels big to your tongue.'

'Ah, me!' sighed Uncle Jack, putting on a funny voice, 'Tongues are terrible things for not telling the truth.'

Granny fetched a piece of tissue paper from the kitchen and wrapped Mary Kate's tooth in it.

'Keep it safely tucked in your pocket,' she said. 'You must take it home and put it under your pillow tonight.'

Mary Kate stared at her. 'Whatever for?' she asked. It seemed a very odd thing to do.

Uncle Jack leaned forward and said, solemnly, 'Because it isn't really your tooth, Mary Kate. It belongs to the fairies. They only lend these tiny teeth to you for a little while. Then they want them back.' He wagged his finger at her. 'Make no mistake, Mary Kate. This is a fairy tooth. The fairies will come for it tonight. And they'll leave you something else in its place.'

'What?' asked Mary Kate. She didn't know whether to believe Uncle Jack or not.

'Wait and see,' said Granny, smiling.

That night, when Mummy was putting her to bed, Mary Kate took the tooth out of her pocket.

'Granny said I must put the tooth under my pillow,' she said. 'Uncle Jack said the fairies will come for it and leave me something else instead. They won't really, will they, Mummy?'

Mummy smiled – the same sort of smile that Granny had smiled. 'Wait and see,' she said.

In the morning, Mary Kate remembered about the tooth the moment she woke up. She slid her hand under her pillow. The piece of tissue paper was still there.

Feeling rather disappointed, Mary Kate pulled it out and began to unfold it. Long before she reached the hard thing in the middle she knew it couldn't possibly be her tiny fairy tooth. It wasn't. It was a shiny, silvery 5p piece.

# *A Spot of Bother*

It was a fine May morning and Mary Kate was up in her bedroom getting ready for school. At least, she should have been getting ready, but she couldn't find her vest. It wasn't on the chair, where it should have been, and it wasn't on the bed. It wasn't even on the floor under the bed, with her yesterday's socks. The socks weren't supposed to be there, so Mary Kate picked them up and took them to the bathroom to put them in the linen basket.

While she was there, she thought she might as well wash. She ran the water and looked for her face cloth. It wasn't on its little hook. It was screwed up in a soggy bundle between the bath taps.

Then Mary Kate remembered she had undressed in the bathroom last night while her bath was running. Mummy had come in and told her to pick her things up off the floor. She had put her blouse in the linen basket because the collar was grubby. Perhaps her vest had been put in there, too. Mary Kate pulled her yesterday's socks out of the basket again and her yesterday's blouse, but her vest wasn't there. She dried her hands and was back in the bedroom before she remembered she had been going to wash. She trotted back to the bathroom.

Mummy came upstairs just as Mary Kate started to clean her teeth.

'Good gracious, aren't you dressed yet?' she cried. 'Time's getting on, you know. Be quick now. I'll come and help you.'

Mary Kate hurried back to her bedroom without putting the top on the toothpaste and pulled open her sock drawer. She was half hoping her vest might be in there, but it wasn't.

'Where's your vest?' Mummy said, all ready to help Mary Kate to get dressed.

'Don't know,' mumbled Mary Kate, sitting on the edge of the bed to put on her clean socks.

Mummy pulled the bedclothes this way and that, looked under the bed, looked on the chair and behind the chair and in the wardrobe and then went across to the bathroom.

'It's not there,' called Mary Kate. 'I've looked.'

'I'm getting you a clean one,' Mummy said, coming back with it. 'There's no time to mess about. You'll be late for school.'

She bundled Mary Kate into her clothes and then started to brush her hair. It was very tangly.

'Whatever were you doing last night?' asked Mummy. 'Your hair's like a bird's nest.'

Mary Kate said nothing. She thought she had better not tell Mummy she had been trying to make her hair into a pigtail, like her best friend Susan's.

Daddy had cleaned Mary Kate's shoes when he cleaned his. They were in the kitchen. Mary Kate ran down and put them on. She was in the hall, wriggling herself into her blazer, when she remembered she had promised Teddy she would take him to school with her today.

She rushed upstairs to fetch him.

'Where are you going now?' called Mummy, hearing her thump across the landing. 'You'll miss the bus if you're not quick.'

'I'm getting Teddy,' shouted Mary Kate, burrowing into the tangle of bedclothes at the bottom of the bed to find him.

Teddy was still in his pyjamas. They were very nice pyjamas. Auntie Mary had made them for him when he went to hospital with Mary Kate. All the same, he couldn't go to school in them. Mary Kate would have to dress him.

She unbuttoned his pyjama jacket. Then she stopped. Under his pyjamas Teddy was wearing Mary Kate's yesterday's vest.

'Come downstairs!' shouted Mummy from the hall. She sounded cross.

'Coming,' called Mary Kate and hastily pushed Teddy to the back of the toy cupboard, vest and all.

Mummy had the front door open, all ready to take Mary Kate up the hill to the bus stop, but they were hardly out of the house when the school bus went by.

'There!' cried Mummy. 'I said you'd miss it, didn't I?'

'I can go the field way, can't I?' said Mary Kate. 'It isn't raining.' When it rained the field path was muddy, especially the bit by the stream.

'You'll have to go by yourself, then,' Mummy told her. 'I can't come with you. I'm expecting the chimney sweep at a quarter to nine.'

All the same, Mummy went with her down the garden to the gate that led into the little wood.

'I'll come as far as the stile,' she said.

When they reached the stile, Mary Kate climbed over, held up her face for a kiss and skipped away across the field.

Mummy stood watching her for a moment, then hurried back to the house. She must have been thinking very hard about something, because she quite forgot to shut the garden gate.

Jacky, the dog, dashed out of the kitchen as soon as Mummy opened the back door. She didn't bother to call him back. She thought he was quite safe, in the garden.

It didn't take Jacky long to find the open gate. Tail wagging, he trotted into the wood, sniffing at the narrow footpath.

Mary Kate had stopped on the bridge, to wait for the ducks. They had all the time in the world, so they didn't hurry themselves. She opened her satchel and took out her packet of mid-morning biscuits. She had just broken one up for the ducks when she heard Jacky barking. He was racing across the field towards her.

Mary Kate knew it would be no use telling Jacky to go home. He wouldn't take any notice of her. She dropped the bits of biscuit into the stream and ran as fast as she could towards the kissing-gate on the other side of the field. Once she was in the churchyard, Jacky couldn't follow her.

By the time Mary Kate reached the tall gate in the churchyard wall, Jacky had squeezed under the kissing-gate and was on the footpath behind her.

Panting, Mary Kate stretched up and wiggled hard at the difficult latch. In another moment she was safe in the churchyard. She was only just in time. Jacky reached the gate as she slammed it shut. He pushed his little black nose through the bars and whimpered. Then he leapt up at the latch and began to bark.

Mary Kate could still hear him barking when she ran into the school playground. She heard him several times during the first part of the morning. Then he stopped. 'He's gone home,' she thought and by midday she had forgotten all about him.

She was washing her hands before school dinner when Susan dashed into the cloakroom. 'Your dog's in the playground,' she said. 'Come and see.'

Out ran Mary Kate – and there was Jacky, being petted and patted by a crowd of giggling children.

He had somehow found his way round to the street and in at the school gate. There was a barrier to stop the children running out into the road, but it couldn't stop Jacky.

As soon as he saw Mary Kate, he rushed at her, barking joyfully.

'You bad dog,' she said, catching him by the collar and trying to make him keep still.

'Is that your dog, Mary Kate?' asked Miss Laurie, coming to see what all the noise was.

'Yes, Miss Laurie,' said Mary Kate. 'He followed me to school this morning.'

'Well, you'd better send him home again,' Miss Laurie said. 'Put him out of the back gate. We don't want him loose in the street, do we?'

'No, Miss Laurie,' said Mary Kate meekly, and led the struggling Jacky across the playground to the back gate. It was a rather rickety old gate and nobody used it now. The path behind it was quite overgrown and full of stinging nettles.

Mary Kate didn't want to push Jacky out on to the weedy path, but Miss Laurie was watching her so there was nothing else she could do.

'Go on, go home,' she said, hoping he would find a hole in the hedge so that he could get into the field beyond.

Jacky whined and barked and jumped up at

the gate as Mary Kate ran back across the playground to have her dinner.

Half-way through the meal, the children at the table near the door began to nudge one another and giggle. Some of them bent down and looked under the table.

Jacky had found his way back into the playground. Now he was in the dining-room, creeping along under the table, looking for Mary Kate.

The children patted his head and fed him with scraps from their plates, keeping one eye on Miss Laurie, who seemed not to have noticed that anything was going on. She was talking to the Dinner Lady and only half watching the children.

Suddenly Jacky found Mary Kate. He tried to get up on to her lap.

'What's happening?' cried Miss Laurie, coming to see. When she saw, she said, 'Oh, it's that dog again, is it? Well, if he won't go away I'm afraid he'll have to be tied up in the boiler house till it's time to go home.'

'Can't Mary Kate take him home?' asked Susan. 'I could go with her. It won't take us long.'

'Certainly not,' said Miss Laurie. 'I can't possibly allow you to go wandering off like that. You're in my charge till going-home time. I'm supposed to keep an eye on you and see you come to no harm.'

She took Jacky firmly by the collar and marched him off towards the boiler house.

Suddenly Mary Kate had an idea. 'Miss Laurie! Miss Laurie!' she shouted, running after her teacher.

'Can I take Jacky to Granny's?' she asked, pointing across the street to the lane where Granny lived. 'You can see her house from the corner of the playground. You'll be able to keep your eye on us.'

Granny *was* surprised when she opened her front door and found Mary Kate and Jacky standing there.

'Whatever next!' she said, when Mary Kate had explained. 'Off you go, now, before you get into any more trouble. I'll take Jacky home this afternoon. Let's hope Mummy hasn't been hunting for him all morning.'

Mary Kate went thoughtfully back to school.

She had a feeling she *was* going to get into more trouble. Even if Mummy hadn't been hunting for Jacky, she had almost certainly been hunting for Mary Kate's yesterday's vest, which Teddy was still wearing.

# A Walk and Aunt Mary

Aunt Mary had come for the week-end. She had arrived on Friday afternoon, just in time to meet Mary Kate from school. Granny was there, too, so Mary Kate walked home the field way with them instead of going on the school bus.

Aunt Mary couldn't stay with Granny when she came to the village because the room she and Mummy shared when they were girls had been turned into a bathroom. The attic was Uncle Jack's room, just as it had been when he and Uncle Ned were boys.

Aunt Mary had a little room in Mary Kate's house. It opened off the dining-room and it had a glass door that led to the path by the side gate, so Aunt Mary could come and go as she pleased.

On Saturday morning Mary Kate and Aunt Mary did all the shopping. They walked to the village and did Mummy's shopping first. Then they called on Granny. They left Mummy's basket in Granny's kitchen while they did Granny's shopping. Aunt Mary said she thought they had earned themselves a special treat, so she took Mary Kate to the Bun Shop for coffee and cakes. Mary Kate's coffee was mostly milk but that was the way she liked it. She had a lovely, squashy, sugary fresh cream doughnut with it. The sugar stuck to her fingers and her face and a blob of cream somehow put itself on the end of her nose, so Aunt Mary had to clean her up with a paper napkin.

'There!' she said, when Mary Kate was more or less clean again. 'Now we'll take Granny her shopping and collect Mummy's and then we'll go home on the bus. I think we've done enough walking for one morning.'

'Don't you like walking?' asked Mary Kate.

'Some kinds of walking,' said Aunt Mary, 'but not trudging about with heavy shopping baskets.'

After lunch Mummy and Aunt Mary sat in the garden for a while and Mary Kate helped Daddy weed the flower border. Then they all tidied themselves and walked across the fields to have tea with Granny.

After tea Granny lit a fire because the evenings were still chilly and Mary Kate sat on Granny's rocking chair and rocked herself. She rocked and rocked and rocked and then she was asleep.

Mummy woke her up at last and said it was nearly time to go home.

'You shouldn't have let her sleep so long,' Granny said. 'She'll be awake half the night.'

By the time they had had supper and walked home the long way round because the field way was too dark, Mary Kate was quite tired again. It was much later than her usual bedtime. She went to sleep almost at once but she woke up very early on Sunday morning. The room was still dark but Mary Kate felt very wide awake, so she thought it must be time to get up. She slid out of bed and pulled back the curtains. It wasn't quite light yet, but all the birds were singing, whistling and trilling, wild and sweet and shrill, in the wood at the bottom of the garden.

'I'm terribly thirsty,' said Mary Kate, to no one in particular. Then she remembered it was Sunday and breakfast wouldn't be for a long time yet. She decided to creep downstairs and get herself a drink of water.

What a surprise she had when she opened the kitchen door! There was Aunt Mary, with her outdoor things on, standing by the draining board drinking a cup of tea.

'Good gracious me!' she said, when she saw Mary Kate. 'You're an early bird. Nearly as early as the ones that woke me up.'

'I want a drink,' Mary Kate said. 'Is it morning or is it still last night?'

'Morning,' Aunt Mary told her, 'but only just. Here, have a cup of tea.'

'Why have you got your coat on?' asked Mary Kate, curling her hands round the warm mug and sipping the sweet milky tea.

'I'm going for a walk,' said Aunt Mary. 'I'm going out to see the day begin. We don't get mornings like this in London – at least, not in the part of London where I live.'

Mary Kate drank her tea fast. 'Can I come

with you?' she gasped, after the last mouthful.

Aunt Mary looked doubtful. Then she said, 'Well, I don't see why not. You're wide awake now so you probably won't go to sleep even if I send you back to bed. I'll go up and fetch your things. No need to wake Mummy and Daddy. Just give your hands and face a quick splash under the tap. You can have a proper wash when we come back.'

By the time Mary Kate had pretended to wash her face and hands, Aunt Mary was downstairs again with her clothes and her hairbrush. She

dressed her quickly, smoothed her hair a bit and put her hat on.

Pussy Pipkin stirred in his basket by the stove, stretched his long front legs, tipped back his head and yawned, licked down his front once, twice – and curled up again for more sleep.

'Where's Jacky?' asked Mary Kate, suddenly realizing he wasn't there.

'Asleep on the bottom of my bed,' said Aunt Mary. 'He thinks I didn't see him sneak in when I came out to put the kettle on.'

'Are we taking him with us? He's not supposed

to sleep on beds,' Mary Kate said.

'I know he isn't,' said Aunt Mary, unlocking the back door, 'but I think we'll leave him there, and go out this way. If we take him out he's sure to start barking and I don't think anybody wants to be woken up by a barking dog at half-past three on a Sunday morning.'

'Is that what time it is?' said Mary Kate, stepping out into the cool morning that hadn't quite started. 'It isn't *nearly* time to get up yet, is it?'

'Not for some people,' said Aunt Mary, 'but it's nearly time for the sun to get up and if we don't hurry we'll miss it.'

She led the way quickly down the garden, through the gate at the bottom and into the little wood. Mary Kate hurried after her. It was creepy dark in the wood. Mary Kate caught hold of the back of Aunt Mary's coat as they went along the narrow path towards the stile.

Once they were in the field, it was lighter.

'Quick,' said Aunt Mary. 'The sky's getting pink already.'

They didn't take the path across the field to the churchyard. Instead, they climbed the

214

sloping ground close to the wood till they reached the top of the hill.

There they stopped, to watch the sun come up. Pink and gold and glowing, burning bright with a splendid light, the day began. Mary Kate thought it was wonderful. She held Aunt Mary's hand and never said a word. Even the birds had hushed their morning noise for this marvellous moment. The sky changed from pale grey to blue and the fiery sun shone straight at Mary Kate, putting pink in her face.

'It's warm,' she said, blinking in the brilliant light. 'I can feel it warm already.'

'It's going to be a lovely day,' Aunt Mary said. 'Come on. Race you down the hill.'

They ran down the other side of the hill through the soaking grass. Now Mary Kate knew why Aunt Mary had told her to put her boots on and not her shoes. Aunt Mary had a funny bag thing hanging from a strap over her shoulder. It was very old and rather shabby. It bumped up and down as she ran, so she pulled it round and held it under her arm.

She slowed down half-way down the hill and

pretended to be quite worn out. Mary Kate reached the far fence first and leaned against it, waiting for Aunt Mary.

'What have you got in that bag?' she asked, breathlessly.

'Things,' said Aunt Mary. 'Two minutes' rest and then we'll go on round by Dingley Wood.'

They didn't go into the wood because it was cool with shadows and Aunt Mary wanted to stay out in the sunlight. They followed the field path all the way along by the chestnut paling fence and peered through the green gloom of the rhododendrons at the dark lines of pine trees beyond.

At the edge of the plantation, the trees were different. This was the old Dingley Wood, or what was left of it. Between the silver birches the ground was misty mauve with bluebells, and rabbit paths criss-crossed the tangled grasses.

'I'm hungry,' said Aunt Mary. 'How about you?'

'*Starving*,' said Mary Kate, but she didn't really want to go home yet, for breakfast.

'Let's go and sit on that tree-trunk,' suggested

Aunt Mary, leading the way into the wood.

The fallen tree-trunk looked like a creature, with its broken leggy branches and sticking-up short snout.

Mary Kate pretended it was a monster and climbed on to its back.

Aunt Mary sat down and opened the knapsack she had been carrying.

'We'll have our picnic now,' she said.

Mary Kate was delighted. It was the first time she had had a picnic breakfast. Aunt Mary had brought a flask of tea, two crusty buttery rolls, three cold sausages, two tomatoes and a bar of chocolate. Mary Kate thought it was quite the nicest breakfast she had ever had.

When they had finished they picked a bunch of primroses to take home to Mummy.

'Shall we take some bluebells?' asked Mary Kate.

'Only one,' said Aunt Mary. 'Just to prove we've been here. Bluebells don't do very well indoors. They don't look right in a vase and they don't live long. They're better left where they are.'

'They don't smell the same indoors, do they?' said Mary Kate, sniffing the delicately scented air. 'They smell lovely out here.'

'That's because there are so many of them here,' Aunt Mary told her.

The church clock struck six as they walked down the rutted cart track towards the lane that led back to the village.

'Mummy won't be up yet, will she?' asked Mary Kate. It felt very odd to be out in the fields while everyone else was in bed. She thought how surprised Mummy would be when she woke up and found no Mary Kate and no Aunt Mary in the house.

'Mummy won't be up for ages,' Aunt Mary said, 'but I expect Granny will. Shall we go and see?'

Granny *was* up. She was making herself a pot of tea when Aunt Mary and Mary Kate peeped through her kitchen window about half an hour later.

'Good gracious me!' she said, opening the door to let them in. 'Have you been out all night?'

'Not quite,' said Aunt Mary. 'We got up to see the sun rise. We just popped in for a cup of tea.'

'You might as well stay to breakfast now you're here,' said Granny.

'We've had our breakfast,' said Mary Kate. 'We had it in Dingley Wood.'

She drank her tea and then wandered off into Granny's parlour. Last night's fire was still alight, a heap of hot grey ashes, with here and there a glowing scrap of coal.

Mary Kate climbed into the rocking chair and began slowly to rock herself to and fro. When Aunt Mary looked in a few minutes later, she was curled up, fast asleep.

# The School Sports

Sports Day had come at last. For weeks Mary Kate had been practising for the egg-and-spoon race with a big spoon and a little potato. She was really quite good at it now.

She had been practising for the flat race, too. Mummy and Daddy had run races with her in the garden. They couldn't help her with the three-legged race, though. Mummy did try, once, just for fun. She and Mary Kate staggered all hunched up and hobble-de-hee across the lawn and fell in a heap on the grass.

'There's going to be an obstacle race,' Mary Kate said, at breakfast on the great day. 'You have to pick up a lot of rings and put them in a basket and dress up in a coat inside out and gloves and a hat and big Wellingtons and crawl through a barrel. I don't think I'll go in for that one. I'm sure I shall get all muddled up.'

'It won't matter,' Daddy said. 'It's only a bit of fun. I should have a go, if I were you.'

'Are you coming, Daddy?' asked Mary Kate. 'Mummy's coming. So is Granny. Lots of daddies are coming.'

'I'll do my best,' Daddy promised. 'It all depends how much work I find waiting for me when I get to the office. If I can possibly get away, I will. I can't be sure I'll be there at the start, but I'll do my best to come before it's all over. Anyway, good luck, poppet.'

He gave Mary Kate a quick kiss and went off to catch his train.

'I hope he can come,' Mary Kate said.

'Well, it *is* Friday,' said Mummy, 'so he's much more likely to be able to get away today than any other day. Anyway, I'll be there to cheer you on. Look out for me right at the start.'

It wasn't easy to settle down to proper lessons that morning. Even the teachers kept looking out of the window to make sure the sun was still shining. There were a lot of last-minute preparations still to be made and everyone was so busy that Miss Laurie quite forgot to blow the whistle after mid-morning break, so there was a longer playtime than usual.

While the children were having their dinners, the parents who had offered to help came to take the chairs and benches from the school to the Sports Field. There were several cars with roof-racks, three small vans, a tractor and trailer and Mr Bean, with his horse and cart. Mr Bean always closed his junk-yard and his second-hand

shop on Sports Day and came to help at the school.

It wasn't long before the benches had been taken out of the school hall and the store room and the chairs out of the classrooms. Then the fun began. As the children finished their dinners, they carried their chairs out into the playground. Each child with a chair was greeted with a cheer from the children by the gate.

Mary Kate loved every minute of it. Most of the children had seen it all before, of course, but to her it was all new and exciting. She watched the cars and the vans drive away with the chairs, and the tractor move slowly off with its trailer-load of long benches. Mr Bean was the last to go.

His horse and cart followed the procession down the lane where Granny lived, past the little fenced-off Green where the swings were, to the Recreation Ground, which was the cricket pitch and the football field and the place where the Fête was held.

At last the time came for the children to go to the Sports Field. They lined up in the play-

ground in a long, long, wriggly crocodile, all wearing their blue shorts and white shirts and carrying their cardigans and pullovers.

Then two of the teachers held up the traffic and the crocodile hurried across the road and down the little lane on the other side. Mary Kate was right in the front, with Susan.

Just as the children reached Granny's cottage, her door opened and she came out.

'There's Granny!' cried Mary Kate, waving her hand. At that, all the other children waved, too. Granny stood at her gate and watched them. She was wearing her best hat and coat, all ready to come and see Mary Kate run in the races.

There were quite a lot of mothers and fathers in the field when the children arrived. Mary Kate looked to see if her Mummy was there, but she wasn't.

'I s'pose Granny's waiting for her,' she said, when Granny didn't appear. Mary Kate had expected her to follow the long line of children down the lane.

It was a lovely day. It hadn't rained for so long that the ground was quite dry and warm. The children sat cross-legged on the short grass, because all the chairs and benches were needed for the parents and friends. The sky was so bright and the sun so hot that Mary Kate began to feel a little sleepy. She closed her eyes.

'There's my Mummy,' said Susan loudly – and woke her up.

It was almost time for the races to start. Miss Chesney was looking at her watch and Miss Laurie was looking at the list of children who were in the first race.

Mary Kate began to feel a little anxious. She screwed up her eyes and looked all round the field. There were the babies in their prams and the toddlers rolling about on the grass. There were the grannies and aunties and mothers, in their gay summer frocks and pretty hats. There were even a few fathers, in flannels and white shirts, with the sleeves rolled up. There was the man from the local paper, with his camera. There were two men in grey suits and panama hats. Mary Kate didn't know who they were. They were talking to the vicar. He was wearing his dark Sunday suit and he looked rather hot.

Miss Laurie blew her whistle. The children stopped chattering.

'First race. Under fives,' said a queer booming voice. It was one of the panama hat men. He was calling through a megaphone.

Mary Kate looked round the field again. She stared at all the smiling faces but the face she wanted to see wasn't there. *Her* Mummy hadn't come.

The next race was the flat race for the five-year-olds. This was Mary Kate's first race. She lined up with the other children, wondering what could have happened to Mummy and Granny.

'Don't look at the people, Mary Kate, or you'll run all crooked,' said Miss Laurie. 'Keep your eye on that big oak at the far end of the field.'

Mary Kate stared miserably at the oak tree. She stared at it so hard she didn't realize she was supposed to start running till she saw the others rush forward. She ran as fast as she could but she didn't win. She trailed across the field behind the others and went back to her place beside Susan.

'Your Gran's just come,' Susan said. 'She's over there. Look.'

Mary Kate looked. There was Granny, standing behind the second row of chairs, waving a scarf at her.

Mary Kate waved back and sat down. She still couldn't see Mummy anywhere but at least there would be somebody there belonging to her to see her run in the other races.

All the flat races were run first. It was a good

arrangement because that way nobody had to run in two races straight off.

Then it was time for Mary Kate's egg-and-spoon race.

She felt much more nervous about this race than she had about the first one. Her hand shook as she stood at the starting line, holding the big metal spoon. The old, rough, wooden egg rolled about in the most alarming way. Mary Kate was sure she was going to drop it.

The other panama hat man was starting the races. He blew one blast on a whistle, very clear and shrill.

'Ready ... steady ... pee-ee-eep,' he went. Off went the children, walking stiffly, looking down at their spoons, trying not to wobble.

Mary Kate was doing very well. She was in third place. Out of the corner of her eye she could see the white line painted on the grass, so she knew she was going straight. She could see the heels of the two children in front, too, but she didn't know who they were.

The people were cheering and calling the children's names.

'Come on, Johnny . . . come on, Sally . . . come on, Susan . . .'

Then, suddenly, loudly, clearly, somebody shouted, 'Come on, Mary Kate!'

It was Daddy! It was Daddy, cheering her on, louder than anybody else. He had come, after all. He must have let Mummy know, somehow, and she had been waiting for him.

Mary Kate almost ran, she was so happy. The spoon jerked in her hand. The egg lurched sideways, tipped to the rim of the spoon, tottered – and rolled back into place. Mary Kate's heart was thumping and her throat was dry. She had almost dropped the egg.

There couldn't be far to go now but she didn't dare look up. There seemed to be no one else on the field – just herself, walking and walking and almost bursting with trying not to drop the precious egg.

All about her voices were calling and they all seemed to be saying the same thing.

'Come on, Mary Kate . . . come on, Mary Kate . . . Mary Kate . . . Mary Kate . . .'

Then it was over. She saw the tape – she

touched it – she heard Miss Chesney's voice say, 'Well done, Mary Kate. My goodness, you *were* fast. It was most exciting.'

Mary Kate smiled and looked past Miss Chesney to the long line of mothers and fathers and aunties and grannies, all smiling and clapping. She was looking for her own Mummy and Daddy and Granny.

There they were, waving to her, hurrying along behind the chairs – Mummy and Daddy and Granny and Uncle Jack and Aunt Mary and Uncle Ned and Auntie Dot.

No wonder there had been so many voices cheering her on. The whole family had come with Daddy to see Mary Kate win her very first race.